Medics, Sisters, Brides

From second chances to forever afters!

Ever since an accident left Abby Phillips wheelchair-bound as a toddler, sister and nurse Annalise has been by her side. The two sisters have been inseparable. But when they each receive a once-in-a-lifetime chance to face the world alone and follow their professional dreams, they decide to seize the moment.

As their adventures unfold, neither are prepared for the romantic roller coaster awaiting them, too!

Look out for Annalise's story in
Awakening the Shy Nurse

And follow Abby's in
Saved by Their Miracle Baby

Both available now!

Dear Reader,

My mother had a big glass jar of buttons and when I was sick and had to stay in bed as a child, I would be allowed to play with the button jar. It kept me happy for hours as I made button "families" and sorted them into groups according to color or size or how many holes they had. Perhaps the satisfaction of finding those links can help explain the pleasure I get from writing stories that are linked in some way.

I chose sisters this time—Lisa and Abby—and I gave them very strong links, not only because they lost their mother early on but because of a terrible accident that left Abby in a wheelchair and Lisa feeling responsible.

They both have a more complicated journey than most to find love, and I hope you enjoy discovering how, and why, their heroes—Hugh and Noah—meet the challenges the Phillips sisters present.

Happy reading.

With love,

Alison xx

SAVED BY THEIR MIRACLE BABY

—

ALISON ROBERTS

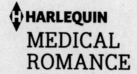

HARLEQUIN

MEDICAL
ROMANCE

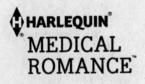

HARLEQUIN®
MEDICAL
ROMANCE™

Recycling programs
for this product may
not exist in your area.

ISBN-13: 978-1-335-14932-9

Saved by Their Miracle Baby

Copyright © 2020 by Alison Roberts

This edition published by arrangement with Harlequin Books S.A.

For questions and comments about the quality of this book,
please contact us at CustomerService@Harlequin.com.

Harlequin Enterprises ULC
22 Adelaide St. West, 40th Floor
Toronto, Ontario M5H 4E3, Canada
www.Harlequin.com

Printed in U.S.A.

Alison Roberts is a New Zealander, currently lucky enough to be living in the South of France. She is also lucky enough to write for the Harlequin Medical Romance line. A primary school teacher in a former life, she is now a qualified paramedic. She loves to travel and dance, drink champagne, and spend time with her daughter and her friends.

Books by Alison Roberts

Harlequin Medical Romance

Rescue Docs

Resisting Her Rescue Doc
Pregnant with Her Best Friend's Baby
Dr. Right for the Single Mom

Hope Children's Hospital

Their Newborn Baby Gift

Twins on Her Doorstep
Melting the Trauma Doc's Heart
Single Dad in Her Stocking

Harlequin Romance

The Baby Who Saved Christmas
The Forbidden Prince

Visit the Author Profile page
at Harlequin.com for more titles.

CHAPTER ONE

IT CAME OUT of nowhere.

A sickening crunch. A thump as the back of Abigail Phillips's head hit the headrest and the car lurched as the engine stalled. The fear that worse was about to come made Abby her screw her eyes shut for a few seconds and grip her steering wheel as if her life depended on it. Was her car going to get hit again and go spinning off into oncoming traffic or the nearest lamppost?

But there was only silence now and her car was just as stable as it had been before the crunch, when Abby had been the first to stop at this red traffic light. She'd only been rear-ended, she realised, and it was probably no big deal. She'd love to jump out of the car and go and inspect any damage to the vehicle that was her pride and joy but that wasn't going to happen. What she did do was take a couple of deep breaths and try to control the way her heart was still hammering against her ribs. Instead of slowing down, however, it completely missed a beat when someone rapped on her window and gave her another fright.

Her eyes flew open. There was a face at her window now. A very concerned-looking face.

'Oh, my God…' she heard him say. 'I'm so sorry. Are you hurt?'

He tried the door but it was locked. Abby wasn't stupid—she knew to lock her door and keep herself safe from something like carjacking. She also remembered some advice she'd heard about never admitting culpability at the scene of an accident because of potential legal ramifications. Either this man had never heard the same advice or he was just too honest not to admit something was entirely his own fault and then apologise for it. Abby liked that enough to make her reach for the switch to lower her window so she could talk to him.

'I'm fine,' she said. He had blue eyes, she noticed. Very, very blue eyes and a tangle of dark lashes that any woman would envy. There were a lot of little creases at the corners of his eyes, too. As if he spent a lot of time smiling. Or focusing on something very small.

He certainly wasn't smiling right now.

'Are you sure? Can I check your neck, at least? I'm a doctor.'

They were only a couple of blocks away from where Abby worked at St John's Hospital so it was quite possible he'd been heading in the same direction. Not that Abby had ever seen him in the hospital corridors or cafeteria. She could be quite sure of that because she would have noticed him. He was rather an attractive man.

Okay…make that *very* attractive. Those intensely blue eyes beneath black hair that was tousled enough to suggest that he didn't bother looking in a mirror very often, along with a bit of designer stubble, was a combination that made it unlikely that Abby's heart rate was going to slow down anytime soon. Especially when he was looking at her like that—as if it was absolutely critical that she wasn't injured.

And then he reached into the car to slide

his hand beneath her long hair, which was loose at the moment, to touch her neck.

'Does this hurt at all?' he asked.

'No…' It didn't hurt. Quite the opposite. She'd never had a man's hand cupping the nape of her neck before, Abby realised, and it felt rather nice. More than rather nice, in fact. He had gentle hands but she could tell he knew exactly what he was doing and it was sending odd little spirals of sensation right down her spine.

Abby wasn't at all sure that it was appropriate to be feeling that tingle when this was the purely professional touch of a doctor checking for a physical injury but it felt like something far more personal. Had she avoided letting any men this close to her for so long she'd forgotten that it *could* be something rather nice?

'Try putting your chin on your chest. Very slowly. Stop if it starts hurting.'

The traffic lights had changed but Abby wasn't going anywhere. A car driver tooted irritably as he pulled out to get around the obstruction the two cars were making. Someone else rolled down their window and shouted.

'Everything okay? Want me to call an ambulance?'

'I think we're okay,' the man shouted back. 'But thank you.' He turned back to Abby. 'Look over one shoulder and then the other. Carefully…'

Abby did as she was told. The second direction sent her gaze back to him.

'No pain?'

'No pain,' she confirmed.

'And nothing else hurting at all? Can you take a deep breath? Oh, God…that's the first thing I should have asked.' His grimace was so like a face palm that Abby almost laughed.

He was so worried about her but she was quite sure she was fine. It had only been a little bump, really, and it probably hadn't even done much damage to her beloved car. The relief came in such a strong wave that Abby felt slightly light-headed. Happy enough to make a joke.

'I really am fine,' she told the stranger. 'Except…'

'Except…?'

'I can't move my legs.' Abby kept a straight face. 'I don't think I'm ever going to walk again.'

The way the colour drained out of his face made her realise that her attempt at humour had backfired.

'Sorry… Maybe I should have said I'll never play the violin again.'

The poor man was looking bewildered now.

'You're supposed to ask if I could play the violin before,' Abby said helpfully. 'And then I say "no" and it's, you know…funny…' It clearly wasn't funny, though, so Abby offered up her brightest smile and used her hand to indicate what was folded up and fitted behind the passenger seat of her modified car.

Her wheelchair.

He wasn't slow, that's for sure. It took only a split second for him to realise that she was paraplegic and that she'd been making a joke about it. His breath came out in a strangled sound—as if he didn't know whether to laugh or cry.

He chose to laugh, albeit shaking his head and catching Abby's gaze at the same time. She could feel her smile stretching into a delighted grin. She was enjoying this, she realised. How inappropriate was that? Especially when she heard the blare of a siren trying to get through traffic that had been slowed down enough to be turning into the kind of traffic jam nobody wanted at peak rush hour. The flashing light of a police motorcycle could be seen threading its way through the traffic and Abby knew there was going to be even more of a hold-up while they sorted this minor accident out.

She was going to be late for work—something that she never allowed to happen—but, strangely, she was actually quite pleased she had an excuse to stay here a bit longer. With the blue-eyed stranger whose face had just become even more attractive when he'd laughed.

Good *grief*... Noah Baxter had just rear-ended the car of some young woman who was already living with a probable spinal injury that had made her paraplegic, standing in the middle of a traffic jam he was responsible for, and he was *laughing* about it?

Not just a wry chuckle either. It was a real laugh that came from somewhere deep in his gut and it felt like...

...it felt like he'd just stepped back in time,

that's what. To a life that was so utterly different to the one he led now. A life where things were funny and tender or stupid and you could simply enjoy the absurdity. Where laughter had been such a normal part of life that he hadn't given it a second thought—never imagining for a moment that even the desire to laugh would be obliterated in a matter of only two terrible days.

A police officer was getting off his bike and coming towards them.

'Anyone hurt here?'

'No.' It was the young woman in the car who spoke first. She still had a twinkle of amusement in her eyes after making that joke about never walking again. Hazel eyes, he noticed now, in a pale face that was framed by long waves of golden red hair. A rather striking-looking woman, in fact. And that smile…it was astonishingly contagious. Noah found himself smiling again as well.

'It was entirely my fault, Officer,' he said. 'I'd been looking for a street sign to make sure I was going the right way and I braked a second too late. Do you need my details?'

The police officer was scanning the road

around them. 'What we need to do is clear this obstruction. Nobody's hurt?'

'No.' Both Noah and the attractive redhead spoke together this time.

'Any damage to the vehicles?'

'I don't think so.' Noah hadn't noticed a bumper lying on the road or anything when he'd rushed to the car in front to see if anyone had been injured. Now he followed the police officer to see that there were only very minor bumps and scratches. No big deal at all.

'No need to write this up, then,' the police officer decided. 'I'm going to start directing the traffic. If you can both move your cars and get going, that would be very helpful.'

Noah nodded. He went back to the car in front. 'There's very little damage,' he said. 'Probably not worth losing a no-claims bonus with our insurance companies for either of us. And there's no reason for the police to be involved.'

'Oh…thank goodness for that. I love this car.'

'He wants us to move our cars and head off asap. Are you sure you're okay?'

'I'm sure. Are you?'

'Yes.' Although there was an odd knot in his gut. Left over from that unfamiliar laughter? Maybe it was also responsible for Noah to do something he hadn't done in more than a decade. 'Can I have your phone number?' he asked. 'Just in case…?'

In case of what? That he'd want to check that symptoms of whiplash hadn't become obvious? Or that her insurance company wouldn't cover the damages if she decided to make a claim? Or…simply because he'd like to see her again? Was her smile this time, as she held his gaze for a heartbeat longer than he might have expected, because she was thinking that she might like to see *him* again?

'Just in case you decide you do want to make an insurance claim and you need my details,' he added hurriedly. He always kept a small notepad in his shirt pocket, with a pen attached. A leftover habit from his days as a junior doctor when there had been just too many things to remember at times and keeping notes of anything important had been vital.

She was telling him her phone number.

And then she turned the key in her ignition and started her car up again.

'Oh…' she said, catching his gaze again as she slid the car into gear, using controls that were attached to her steering wheel. 'My name's Abby, by the way.'

'Noah,' he responded. He was smiling again, too, as he slipped the notepad back into his pocket and got into his own car. How weird was this? He'd had a stupid, thankfully minor, accident that was a disruption he certainly didn't need on his way to a meeting with the new colleagues he would be working with in a matter of days and yet it felt like the best thing that had happened to him in quite a while? Like…a few years?

The police officer was overruling the traffic lights to direct vehicles. He waved Abby through the intersection but then put his hand up to stop Noah going through yet. He watched Abby's car getting further and further away and then the indicator went on and she turned, disappearing from his line of sight.

He still had the remnants of that knot in his gut.

Yeah…it was weird all right…

* * *

The routine was so well rehearsed, Abby could go through the steps without even thinking about it. Her disabled parking slot, on the ground floor of the hospital's parking building, was extra wide, which made it easy to open her driver's door and leave it wide open. The special controls on the central console allowed her to move the car seats. She could tilt the back of her own seat and then pull the passenger seat forward to make it easy to lift out the folded frame of her chair to put it on the ground beside her door.

The wheels, which were removed for transport, came out next and Abby clicked them back into place, pulled the bar at the back of the chair that unfolded it and then locked the brakes on.

It took less than sixty seconds after that to manoeuvre the chair into the best position, put the cushion on the seat, sling her shoulder bag over a push handle, lift her legs out of the car and then, with one hand on the cushion of the wheelchair and the other on the car seat, Abby used her upper body strength to swing herself into her chair. She pressed the remote to lock her car as she turned her chair and started rolling towards the parking building's exit. She was ready for her work day and she was only a few minutes late, despite the delay caused by that minor accident.

Abruptly, Abby stopped and then swung her chair to go back to her car. How on earth had she forgotten to go and check the damage? Because she'd been thinking about a pair of dark, blue eyes with crinkly corners, perhaps, and that tingle of *something* she'd felt when they'd met her own gaze, not to mention that other tingle that his hand on her neck had generated? About a name that was unusual enough for him to be the first Noah she'd ever met? Wondering how soon he might ring her?

She would know it was him as soon as he spoke because his voice was etched into her memory as well. Abby could hear an echo of his voice right now, telling her that there was very little damage to her car as she inspected the rear bumper. He was right, there was only a scratch or two and one small dent that she traced with her fingers. It really wasn't going to be worth either the hassle of the paperwork or losing any discount in the cost of her insurance policy.

It wasn't the first ever scratch in that shiny red paintwork. She'd had the car for over two years now after all, and Abby had knocked the side more than once with the frame of her wheelchair but she still needed to get less precious about this vehicle. The problem was that it had been—and still was—such a big deal in her life.

Her older sister, Lisa, had gone into huge debt to cover the massive cost of a car with the kind of modifications Abby needed because she'd understood how life-changing it would be to have this kind of independence. She would also understand how unsettling it was to have been involved in an accident. She took a photo of the damage and texted it to Lisa.

Oops. Got rear-ended at a traffic light. Not the best way to start my day, huh?

Lisa's response pinged in almost instantly.

OMG. U ok??

All good. Need to get to work now. Will come down and see you later.

Come now. Just to be on the safe side.

Both Lisa and her husband worked in St John's Hospital's emergency department now, although Lisa would be leaving before too long to start her maternity leave. Abby loved both her sister and her brother-in-law dearly but she wasn't about to go and visit them. She had far too much work of her own to get on with. She shouldn't have sent the message at all—she could have told Lisa about it later—but maybe she was still a little shaken up and had needed to touch base with her only family.

No need. Stop…

Abby found a picture icon she'd used in the past—a little helicopter. It was a private code that told Lisa she didn't need a parent any more, especially of the hovering and overprotective type. She followed it with a smiley face, however.

Lisa had been a parent to her all her life.

Six years older than Abby, she'd filled in the gaps left by a mother who had been unable to cope and had then died, leaving a grandmother to step in. It can't have been easy for either of them after the accident that had left Abby in a wheelchair when she'd been little more than two years old. For good measure, Abby added a heart to finish her message.

She propelled herself out of the elevator, through the doors of the parking building and onto the footpath. She was reaching to push the button that would activate the lights for the pedestrian crossing when someone beat her to it.

'Let me do that for you, love.'

It was never going to go away completely, was it? That beat of awareness of what could happen when a man assumed that her lack of physical ability gifted him the opportunity to take total control. She'd learned to deal with it, of course. To subdue fear and protect herself by becoming even more fiercely independent and not worrying about bruising anyone's feelings by rejecting unwelcome advances. She'd even learned to do it quite politely so she bit back a retort that, actually, her hands worked perfectly well, which was why she was using a manual rather than an electric wheelchair, and instead she gave the man a tight smile, her sweet tone disguising a slightly sarcastic thank-you.

He was probably in his early forties, wearing jeans and a T-shirt under a jacket and carrying a laptop bag. It must be her morning for good-looking men, Abby decided, although this one had blond hair and looked like he might enjoy spending his downtime surfing or skiing or something. Anyway… she preferred dark hair. Especially with blue eyes…

The lights changed and Abby moved onto the pedestrian crossing. To her dismay, the man walked out ahead of her holding up one hand, not unlike the police officer who'd overridden the traffic lights to clear the jam, as if the drivers might be considering taking off before the lights went green again and running a poor defenceless disabled person over. It was obviously done to be of assistance to Abby but it made her feel like everybody was staring at her and unwanted assistance had always been a pet peeve from a very early age. One of Abby's earliest memories was trying so hard to climb into a swing and pushing her sister's helping hands away.

'Go 'way. I can do it by myself...'

It was nothing like someone taking sexual advantage of her disability, of course, but it was on the same spectrum as far as Abby was concerned, and while she had learned to deal with the aftermath of that appalling incident, it was never going to be forgotten.

She sped up on the other side of the road, eager to disappear into the steady stream of people already heading into what was a large, busy regional hospital, but the blond man was keeping pace.

'Hey…could I buy you a coffee or something?'

'No.' Her negative response came out as being curt this time. Rude enough to make Abby feel a little ashamed of herself so she offered another tight smile. 'Thanks, but no thanks. Don't think my boyfriend would approve.'

'Oh…' He looked comically disappointed. 'I should have guessed. See ya.'

Not if I see you first, Abby thought, but she let her breath out in a sigh as she took the corridor that led both to the hand clinic

and, further on, to the emergency department. She didn't have a boyfriend—it was
just one of the more polite ways she had to
brush off any interest that men showed in
her. Especially men who saw her disability
before they saw anything else about her.

She hadn't brushed that Noah off, though,
had she? She'd not only given him her phone
number, the thought that he might ring her
was creating an unfamiliar ripple of sensation that was…oh, help…embryonic excitement? Whatever it was, it was enough for
Abby to fish in her shoulder bag to retrieve
her phone as soon as she reached the clinic.
It was also enough to feel disappointed that
she hadn't missed any messages or calls yet
and that, no, her phone wasn't on silent.

It had been a very, very long time since
she'd felt that "waiting for a call" anxiety but
it only took Abby a matter of moments to put
two and two together about why she wanted
to hear from the man who'd driven into the
back of her car this morning. He hadn't seen
her disability, had he? He'd been shocked to
see her wheelchair, which meant that when
he'd met her, he hadn't been influenced by

any kind of social stereotyping or personal prejudice about disabled people.

He'd only seen *her*. Abby Phillips. A specialist hand therapist, which was something she was very proud of being, although he didn't know that yet. Mind you, she was also a twenty-six-year-old virgin, which Abby was definitely not proud of being, but thank goodness she was the only person who knew that.

And why on earth had it occurred to her to think of *that* right now?

Abby opened her locker to get her white coat off the hook and then she went to the mirror to brush her hair and scrape it up into a ponytail that wouldn't get in the way of her work this morning. It was the touch of her own thumbs on the back of her neck that gave her the answer to that question. Because she was thinking of the touch of someone else's hands on her neck. Of how it had made her feel. She wanted Noah to call because she was attracted to him. Possibly more attracted than she'd ever been to anyone else. Ever…

Could this possibly be, perhaps, a case of love at first sight?

Abby caught a glimpse of the grin on her face as she turned away from the mirror.

A kind of "watch this space" grin…

Talk about being thrown in at the deep end.

It was specialist hand surgeon Noah Baxter's first day on the job at St John's Hospital and his very first call was to the emergency department for a serious injury to someone's hand. He'd met quite a few of the senior members of his departmental staff the other day but this was his first visit to the ED. The first person he encountered was a nurse who was obviously quite well along in her pregnancy. She greeted him with a friendly smile.

'Can I help you?'

'I've been paged for a consult. By a Hugh Patterson?'

The nurse's smile widened. 'I know him well. I'll let him know you're here.' She turned and went swiftly in the direction of one of the closed resuscitation rooms.

A tension he hadn't actually been aware of started to recede the moment she turned her back. It wasn't anything to do with meeting new colleagues or not knowing what he'd been asked to come and see. It was just that he still hadn't got to a stage when he could see a pregnant belly and not feel a pang of loss. Maybe he never would, but he'd become very good at distracting himself by deliberately noticing something else.

It was her hair that snagged his attention now. Red hair, quite dark. Nothing like that vibrant red gold shade on the woman whose car he'd bumped into the other day on the way to his first visit to St John's. That shade of hair had proved quite memorable.

Too memorable.

Which was why he hadn't yet called that number he'd requested from her. He'd intended to, of course, on more than one occasion in the last few days but when he'd been about to press the call button, he'd just been unable to do it.

Because he really wanted to…

Which was quite ridiculous. He was a single man in his mid-thirties. If he was attracted to a woman he shouldn't be short of the confidence to do something about that. But that was the whole problem, wasn't it?

He *was* attracted to someone. For the first time in years. And he didn't want to be, any more than he wanted to be affected by seeing a pregnant belly. He never wanted to be attracted to anyone again because he knew where that road could lead. Been there, done that and once was more than enough.

Still, it was inexcusable that he hadn't made contact yet and, at the very least, given her his insurance company details. He didn't actually need to ring and hear her voice for that either. He could simply text her the details and he would do that, Noah decided—just as soon as he had a moment to spare later today.

One of the department's consultants emerged from the resuscitation room and strode swiftly towards Noah.

'Hugh Patterson,' he introduced himself. 'And you're Noah Baxter, yes?'

'Indeed.' He shook Hugh's hand.

'We're delighted to have you at St John's. The word is that you're the best in the field. I think that's what our patient might need today.'

Noah raised an eyebrow. 'No pressure, then?'

Hugh's smile had a grim edge. 'Come and see. Not pretty. Patient's a thirty-eight-year-old gentleman who got his hand caught in some food-processing machinery a couple of hours ago. Crush injury to several fingers and partial amputation to his thumb. It took a while to get him free. And it's his dominant hand.'

"Not pretty" was a good description for what Noah found when he lifted the dressings on the man's hand. His fingers and—more importantly—his thumb were all mangled enough for it to be impossible to tell exactly what was, or was not, salvageable, despite the help of the X-rays illuminated on the screen behind the head of the bed. Even if bones could be wired or plated together, there might be too much damage to nerves, tendons and tissues to make reconstruction possible.

'I can't look.' The patient, Steve, had his head firmly turned away and his uninjured hand shielding his eyes. 'Don't touch it...' His breath came out in a sob, '*Please* don't touch it...'

Noah glanced at Hugh. 'He's got a good level of sedation and ten milligrams of morphine on board. Might need a top-up?'

'I'll be as gentle as I can be, Steve,' Noah

told him. 'And I don't need to do much at the moment other than assess what's going on with your blood vessels and nerves. I can already see that we need to take you up to Theatre and get things cleaned up. I'm just going to touch your wrist, here, and the palm of your hand, okay? I want to see what's happening with the blood supply.'

'I can't lose my hand, Doc…' Steve sounded desperate now. 'I can't lose my job. I've got three kids and it's hard enough as it is…'

'I know…' Noah's tone was gentle. 'Try not to panic, Steve. We're going to do everything we possibly can to save your hand, okay?'

He put his fingers on Steve's wrist to occlude the radial and ulnar arteries at the same time as he squeezed gently on the palm of the badly injured hand. Releasing one artery at a time give him good information about the patency of important vessels. Even while he was conducting this test, Noah was gathering other impressions. The colour and temperature of this hand was poor compared to Steve's uninjured hand, which meant that the sooner they got him to Theatre the better to debride these injuries and repair blood vessels. An inadequate blood supply could mean complications in delayed healing, fibrosis and infection.

With the injured hand covered again with sterile dressings, an operating theatre being set up, additional assistance from orthopaedic, vascular and neurosurgical staff requested and Steve's panicked wife arriving in the department with a baby in her arms, Noah had a few minutes to pull up a chair, introduce himself properly and talk through what he was going to do.

'So we'll do our very best to save whatever we can,' he finished up. 'Especially with your thumb because it's so important in achieving useful function of your hand, but we won't know how much we can do until we can see exactly what the damage is. And there are risks, as I've explained. Are you happy to sign the consent form or do you have any more questions?'

Steve's wife, Pauline, was still looking terrified. 'They told me when I arrived that you're the best in the country for hand surgery, Mr Baxter. One of the best in the world so we'll leave it up to you.'

Steve had his uninjured hand covering his

eyes again and his voice was choked. 'I need my hand,' he managed. 'How am I going to be able to work, otherwise? Or look after my family…?'

Pauline shifted the baby to one arm as she reached to touch Steve's shoulder. 'We'll manage, babe,' she told him. 'I'm sure Mr Baxter is going to be able to save your hand…' Her glance at Noah was a plea that was made even more eloquent as this young couple's baby began crying as she turned back to her husband. 'But whatever happens, we're going to get through this. I love you…'

'You'll have to sign the form for me,' Steve was clutching his wife's hand now and there were tears on his cheeks. 'You know how useless I am with my left hand…'

He was confident, that's for sure, but maybe that came with the territory of being renowned as the best in the field.

Fancy being about to start your first surgery in a new hospital, leading a large team of people he'd only just met, and this Mr Baxter had given permission for the gallery to be open. Word had spread like wildfire, of course, but staff in the hand clinic were well up in the priority list, and Abby had been thrilled that she could go and watch because her next appointments were with inpatients and they could be fitted in later in the day. She was more than happy to skip her lunch break, if necessary, to compensate.

That the operating theatre gallery had rather steep stairs could have been an issue but one of the orthopaedic registrars, Alex, who was in the clinic when the news came through, had smiled at her.

'Let's go early,' he'd suggested. 'And get the good seats up front.'

Abby appreciated the unspoken part of his suggestion—that they could tuck her wheelchair out of the way before there were too many people around to notice and that Alex would carry her up the awkward entrance to the gallery that had certainly not been built with disabled access in mind. This wasn't the kind of self-important and uninvited assistance like someone directing traffic on her behalf. This was help that was there automatically from someone who knew her well. Someone who knew how much she loved watching the initial repair on a hand

she might well end up working on herself
further down the track.

So, here she was, in a front row seat that
gave her a great view into the theatre below,
where there were at least a dozen people
busy setting up for what would undoubtedly
be complex and lengthy surgery. Abby had
a clear view of one of the television screens,
too, which would give a close-up view of
the microsurgery needed to repair tendons,
blood vessels and nerves.

The patient had been anaesthetised and
was lying with his arm and hand positioned
on a side wing of the operating table. Nurses
and registrars were busy making sure that
everything was ready for the stars of the
show—the surgeons. There were trays of in-
struments being checked, lights being positioned and headsets with both cameras and
magnifying technology being readied.

All they needed now was the lead surgeon
and he came in from the scrub room, already
gowned and masked, with his gloved hands
crossed in front of him to prevent him touching anything not sterile.

He nodded towards the team of people waiting to work with him and then he

glanced up towards the gallery. Just the briefest glance that raked the packed seating available and acknowledged the people who were interested in what he was about to do. Only his eyes were visible because he hadn't yet had the headgear placed but there was something familiar about his face that made Abby frown as she tried to focus more clearly.

'Who's that?' she asked Alex. 'Mr Baxter or one of the orthopaedic guys?'

'Yep... Noah Baxter. Let's hope he's as good as they say he is.' Alex glanced up at the screen above them, which was filled with the close-up image of the mangled fingers. 'That hand's a mess.'

A bit like Abby's head right now, then, and it was going to take a breath or two for her to get it back under control. Her excitement at being able to observe such major surgery had evaporated. Replaced by something that should have been anger but, pathetically, felt much more like a surprisingly sharp disappointment.

Noah...of course it was. She would never forget those eyes.

She hadn't been about to forget him at all, for that matter. *Or* forgive him.

He hadn't called her. He had probably never even intended to.

CHAPTER TWO

HE COULDN'T HAVE missed that hair.

Not in a million years. Certainly not when she was sitting in the front row of this operating theatre's gallery because the edge of the pool of light over the central table reached far enough to catch the golden glint and make it shine like some kind of halo.

It hadn't seemed like a big deal when he'd agreed to have the gallery open. Noah was quite used to having colleagues, medical students or other interested staff members who worked in the field observing his work but the last person he would have expected to see was the woman he'd met when he'd bumped her car the other day.

The woman who'd made him laugh...

Abby.

Not that he was about to wonder why on

earth she was here, acknowledge her in any way, or let her presence interfere with his focus on his work, but…in the split second before he shut it down, Noah was aware of a beat of something like dismay. Embarrassment, even, because he hadn't yet followed up after that accident to give her those insurance company details or check that she hadn't shown any symptoms of injury later.

There was nothing he could do about that right now, however, so Noah had to dismiss it as completely irrelevant. He had a microphone, as well as the magnifying lens and the camera that would transmit the close-up images to the screens, built into his headset. There were plenty of people other than Abby who would be listening to everything he said and Noah enjoyed both teaching and explaining what he was doing for the nonsurgeons in his audience.

'This thirty-eight-year-old gentleman had an altercation with machinery approximately two hours ago. We know there were no cutting blades involved or any belts or chains, no exposure to extreme heat, cold or chemicals, and the extrication was time-consuming but fortunately without major blood loss so our patient is haemodynamically stable.

'We now have to convert a dirty and contaminated wound into a clean surgical field. We're doing this, firstly, by using a solution of saline, iodopovidone and hydrogen peroxide. I'm also a fan of rigorous scrubbing with a brush, keeping in mind that our aim is to get the wounds clean with the least possible amount of tissue damage.'

He had registrars and nurses helping with this decontamination and Noah realised he hadn't quite shut down that awareness of that particular member of his audience. That would change very soon, however. He was not only extremely well practised in a focus on his work that shut out anything else in the world, he had used it as his personal salvation for years. Nothing was about to undermine that ability.

'The second step of creating our clean surgical field is a meticulous and thorough debridement of any non-viable tissue, foreign bodies, shredded tendon pieces or avulsed nerve and also any bone pieces that don't have an attachment to tendon or muscle. Have a look at the way the fingers are lying, here.' He touched the tips of the fingers, which were lying flat. 'You can see from the disruption to the cascade position of progressively more flexion in the fingers that we're dealing with some damage to the flexor tendons.'

This was it. He was well into the zone of being unaware of anything irrelevant. He was still capable of keeping his audience informed at every step, however, no matter how long the surgery was going to take.

'The fractures of the index and small fingers are so comminuted I'm going to use mini-external fixators. These will be removed in about six weeks…'

'The best way to achieve a precise reduction of the fracture in this finger is a low-profile ladder plate…'

'The thumb is our main concern, here. The primary aim for the treatment of any hand injuries is for our patient to end up with a functioning hand and, as I'm sure you all know, the opposition and pincer mechanism and the sensation for grasping are the most important aspects for useful function. Fortunately, our man is not diabetic and is a nonsmoker, which is to his advantage as far as healing is concerned.'

The thumb was, unfortunately, the most seriously injured part of this hand and could well need further surgery, including tendon transfers. The blood vessel and nerve repairs were also more challenging and Noah was happy to work alongside the specialists that were already a part of St John's surgical staff.

After a long, tiring stint in Theatre, he had a lot of people to thank. He knew they would be playing catch-up with their own workload for the rest of the day, having taken the time to assist with this emergency surgery.

For his own part, Noah stayed in Theatre to supervise the splinting of Steve's hand and arm. He knew the gallery was emptying above them but he could sense how slow it was, with people wanting to chat as they filed out of the tiered seating towards the doors. He wanted to look up. Now that the surgery was completed, the questions were filtering back into his mind.

Why was Abby here?

How, exactly, had she managed to use those stairs to get into a front row seat?

He got the answer to that question as he followed his patient's bed out of the double doors towards Recovery. Stripping off his gloves and mask to ball them up in one hand, a sideways glance showed Abby being lowered into her wheelchair from the arms of a young man. As she positioned her feet on the footplate and unlocked her brakes, the man who had been carrying her stepped aside and she looked up—straight towards Noah.

No…make that glaring, rather than looking, but she broke the eye contact almost instantly. Her chin rose and she swivelled her chair and took off. The determined push of her hands as eloquent as any signal of dismissal.

Noah could feel a bit of an internal cringe going on.

'Who's that?' he asked his registrar. 'In the wheelchair?'

'Abby Phillips. One of the therapists in the hand clinic. Don't be fooled—that chair doesn't stop her doing anything. She's one of the best.'

Noah simply gave a single nod to acknowledge the information. Or maybe it was his agreement that she could probably do anything she chose to do. He didn't say anything because he was thinking too hard. As a specialist hand therapist, Abby was going to be an important part of the team of people he would be working with. It was all very well to repair hands with clever surgery but it was the aftercare and especially the therapy his patients received that could determine the success of their outcomes.

He could very well be working closely with Abby before long and he would undoubtedly need to speak to her, probably in the very near future, so it was unfortunate that she was clearly not going to be happy to see him again. His potential excuse of having mislaid that piece of paper with her phone number on it was not going to cut the mustard, was it?

Maybe some flowers would help?

Noah stepped into the specialised recovery area to help settle his patient for the intensive monitoring he would need as the anaesthetic wore off completely. Steve's wife would be able to come in soon and Noah could give them both the good news that he hadn't had to amputate any of his fingers but also a warning that only time would tell how well the thumb would be able to heal.

A last thought about Abby slipped into his head before he refocused to check the limb baselines on Steve's hand. Flowers were inappropriate because, even with his briefest acquaintance of Abby Phillips, Noah could be quite certain that she wasn't the kind of woman who might be impressed by tokens like flowers or chocolate as a form of apology. She was...*different* and he would have to come up with something a lot more original if he wanted to make amends.

This was good.

Exactly what Abby had needed.

She could feel perspiration trickling down between her shoulder blades, the muscles in her arms were screaming a protest and she was gasping for breath but Abby wasn't about to slow down—especially when her peripheral vision showed how quickly her opponents were closing in on her.

The effort it took to propel a wheelchair with one hand while dribbling a basketball with the other was huge. Which was why this activity was what Abby had needed so badly after her work day. The shock of discovering that the man who had rear-ended her car was the rock star specialist surgeon that they had been so delighted to have attracted to St John's had been overwhelming.

No. It had been crushing, that's what. And it had had nothing to do with his profession. The crushing had been gradual but relentless over the last few days, being added to bit by bit each time she checked her phone and with each extra day that had gone by without Noah calling her. Had she really thought she'd been attracted enough to the man to believe she might look back on that encounter and tell her future children that it had definitely been a case of love at first sight?

At least the aftermath of the final blow to that cringeworthy notion—that he'd never intended to call her at all—had been firmly dispatched by the physical exertion and need for absolute focus on this fast-moving game of wheelchair basketball.

Needing a bit more speed and a change of direction, Abby put the ball on her lap. She could now use both hands to manoeuvre the chair for two pushes before she had to dribble the ball again, pass it to another member of her team or attempt to shoot a goal. She could feel the rise of tension around her and the increase in decibels from encouragement being yelled. Someone grabbing the push ring of her sports chair's steeply cambered wheel prompted a split-second decision and Abby took the ball in both hands, before she could be pulled off her line, aimed for the hoop and put every ounce of her remaining energy into trying to score a goal.

The cheer from the team's substitutes on the side of the court was the best sound Abby had heard all day. She'd done it. Scored a goal from outside the semi-circle around the opposing team's basket, which made it a three-point goal. It meant, that in the last seconds of the fourth and final ten-minute session of the match, she had taken her team to a win.

'Way to go, Abby!'

There was a lot of shouting and cheering from the audience in this gymnasium as well, but there was one voice she could recognise amongst them. Lisa had come with Abby to watch the match tonight. As soon as Abby had showered and changed she was going to drive Lisa back to her house, stopping to pick up a takeout meal on the way. A once-a-week, easy meal together for the sisters had become a family tradition ever since Abby had moved out of the house she'd shared with Lisa after their grandmother's death. They took turns with whose house they went to. They also took turns to choose which variety of food.

'It's my turn to choose,' Lisa announced as Abby came out of the changing rooms, still combing her loose hair with her fingers to help it dry. 'I'm craving Thai food. Or possibly pizza.'

'I think you'll find it's my turn,' Abby countered. 'And I want fish and chips.'

Lisa laughed. 'No, you don't. What you really want is just the chips and mushy peas and gravy.'

Abby nodded. 'This is true but I deserve it. Apart from winning this game, my day kind of sucked.'

'Oh? How come?'

'It's a long story and I need food. Possibly wine. It's Friday night, after all.'

'I guess that swings the vote to fish and chips. There's a wine shop right beside the chippie.' But Lisa looked thoughtful. 'There's a pizza place there as well and we do need to get extra food. I just got a text from Hugh to say he'd invited someone home for a drink after work and they're still there. You don't mind that it's not just us, do you?'

'Of course not. But let's go. I'm starving.'

'Where's your sports chair?'

'Coach is bringing it.' Abby led the way to her car. 'If you can open the hatch, that would help. I'll get myself sorted.'

She was in the driver's seat with her folded wheelchair stowed when the team coach came out with the angled sports wheelchair. He lifted it into the back hatch of her car.

'That was an awesome game, Abby. I still wish you'd think about trying out for the Paralympic team.'

Abby shook her head. They'd had this conversation before—privately. 'You know how important my job is to me and I just don't have the time for the extra training or travel.'

She had to have the conversation all over again with Lisa as they headed home and explain that, as much as she loved her sport, she loved her work even more and she wasn't going to jeopardise either her position in such a great clinic or the progression of her skills. It was almost turning into an argument by the time she pushed herself up the ramp that Lisa and Hugh had installed by the front steps of their gorgeous old country house.

'But surely you could do both?'

'I don't *want* to do both.'

'Hey…' Hugh came out of the kitchen to meet them. He took the pizza boxes off Abby's lap. 'What are you two arguing about?'

'Abby's coach wants her to try out for the Paralympic team.'

'Wow…' Hugh turned to take the wrapped parcels of fish and chips from Lisa.

'I'm not going to do it.' Abby did not appreciate what felt like building pressure. Plus she was very hungry after all that exercise. Hangry, that's what she was. She pushed ahead of both Hugh and Lisa to roll swiftly into the enormous kitchen of this old house, which was where they always ate.

And there, standing in front of an ancient Welsh dresser that had shelves laden with old blue and white china as well as random ornaments and photos, with a beer in his hand and looking quite at home was Noah Baxter.

'Oh…no… Not *you* again…'

Hugh was right behind Abby. 'You two know each other?'

Noah was looking as appalled as Abby's tone had been. 'Ah…we've met,' he said cautiously.

'Yeah…' Abby's breath came out in a huff that didn't quite reach laughter. 'You could say we bumped into each other the other day.'

She was still holding Noah's gaze so she saw the flash that acknowledged the humour in her words. Not that he was about to laugh but she could remember exactly what it had sounded like when he *had* laughed the other day, as easily as she could remember how it had made his face light up. Unfortunately she could also remember just how attracted she had been at that point.

'Oh…*no*…' Lisa echoed Abby's first reaction. 'Don't tell me it was that accident you had on the way to work?'

'Yep.' The only good thing about this incredibly awkward situation was that Abby hadn't told her sister about that instant crush she had developed. Or admitted that she'd been obsessively checking her phone like some dreamy teenager ever since.

Hugh was the first one to actually laugh. 'I had no idea,' he said. 'There I was just being welcoming to a new staff member that I'd only met this morning. But maybe this is a good thing. You can both kiss and make up before you have to work together.'

Abby had to avert her gaze swiftly. The very idea of kissing and making up was… oh, help…something she had no intention of thinking about right now, although she had a feeling it might very well come back to haunt her later.

Hugh put the food down on the big, wooden table and then shifted a chair out of the way for Abby. 'Come and dig in,' he said. 'While it's still hot. Abby, can I get you a glass of wine?'

'What do mean, work together?' At least Lisa had forgotten about the coach's encouragement for Abby to take her sport to the next level. She was staring at Noah. 'You were called in for a consult this morning, weren't you? For that guy with the awful hand injuries?'

'This is Noah Baxter,' Hugh told his wife. 'St John's new specialist hand surgeon. We got so busy after that I never got a chance to tell you.'

'Mmm.' Abby took the glass of wine Hugh had poured for her. 'The famous Mr Baxter. I couldn't believe it was you when I saw you walk into Theatre.'

'And I couldn't believe it was you when I saw you in the front row of the gallery.'

'You got to watch the surgery?' Hugh sounded envious. 'Lucky you.'

Noah was on the other side of the table now and this time he was the one to catch and hold her gaze. Neither of them responded to Hugh's comment. Abby could feel the muscles around her eyes tightening.

You asked for my number... And then you didn't call me...

I know... I'm sorry...it was unforgivable...

The silent exchange made a little shiver run down Abby's spine. Who did that? How could you hear words that hadn't even been spoken like that? Or had he said them out loud? No, she was sure he hadn't—it was just a coincidence that Hugh was giving Noah a sympathetic glance.

'Don't worry, mate. She'll forgive you before too long. It's not as if any real damage was done. It wasn't worth even thinking about making an insurance claim.'

Abby wasn't so sure about no damage having been done but she wasn't thinking about her car.

Noah was making a face as he sat down opposite Abby. 'I was trying to think up something I could put on Abby's desk by way of another apology,' he confessed. 'But I didn't think flowers or chocolates would cut the mustard.'

Abby sneaked a quick glance at him as he took a plate from Lisa. His assessment was correct. But how could he have been so sure that she wouldn't have been impressed with flowers or chocolates? The same way that he could send such an eloquent message with a glance, perhaps?

'The only thing I could think of,' Noah continued, 'was maybe a punching bag with a photo of my face on it.'

That did it. Or maybe it had been those first sips of her wine. Whatever it was, the antagonism in the room evaporated as Abby laughed and Noah grinned at her. Something else took the place of the angst and it was a little disturbing to realise that it was probably the flames of that crush flickering back into life. It was a feeling that got stronger as the group started to relax over their casual meal and Noah became less and less of a stranger. He was watching, fascinated, as Abby piled her plate with hot chips and lined up her small pots of mushy peas and gravy to dip them in.

'I see you're into healthy food, then?'

'Says the man who's stuffing his face with a pizza that has four different types of cheese on it. That's a heart attack on a thin crust.'

'I'll burn it off. Not that I've found any good local running tracks yet.'

'Where are you living?' Lisa asked.

'I've been given a room in the staff quarters for now. I want to get properly settled into my new job before taking any time out to hunt for real estate.'

'It must be something about working exclusively with hands,' Lisa said to Hugh.

'What must?'

'Refusing to take time away from work to do other important things. Like finding a home. Or exploring a sporting talent that could be so brilliant you might win a gold medal on a world stage.'

'Oh…don't start that again,' Abby groaned. 'I'm not going to try out for the Paralympic team. I'm exactly where I want to be, doing exactly what I want to do. Basketball is just my sport. Exercise. Stress relief.'

'Oh…that's right. You said your day had sucked. What happened?'

Oh…help… Abby concentrated on loading mushy peas onto her chip so that she could avoid catching Noah's glance.

'It just got overly busy for a while,' she muttered. 'But that's what happens when you sneak off to watch some complex surgery.'

If Noah had guessed that he was the reason Abby had told her sister that she'd had a bad day, he gave no sign of it now. In fact, he was ready to offer his support.

'I totally get the fascination with working with hands,' he said. 'Obviously. It's an extraordinary field to be in. I couldn't imagine taking time away to do anything else.'

'Really?' Hugh was interested. 'I love the variety of the work I get in Emergency and never knowing what body part is going to come in needing treatment next. Maybe I just have a low boredom threshold.'

'Nothing boring about hands,' Noah said.

'Not that I'm into the kind of inspirational quotes that you see everywhere these days, but I do have a framed quote that I keep on the wall of my office. From a German philosopher, Immanuel Kant.'

'Oh…' Abby's eyes widened. 'I bet I know which one.'

And then they both spoke together.

'*The hand is the visible part of the brain.*'

Oh…this time the exclamation was silent. Because the sudden feeling of connection was a little overwhelming. Noah understood, didn't he? He had the same passion.

Hugh and Lisa shared a look. 'We're going to hear all about the magic of opposable thumbs again, aren't we?'

Noah's lips twitched. 'Well…half of all hand functions do require the thumb.'

'And, apart from the brain, what other body part can do so much?' Abby added. 'And perform such complex tasks? They let us create art and play music, read Braille if you need to or talk with sign language. Hands—and arms—are far more important than legs and feet.' Her voice trailed off as she realised she was preaching to the converted. 'They can give you your independence…'

She could feel the intensity of the look Noah was giving her without lifting her gaze to meet it.

'I'm not surprised to hear that you're so good at your job,' he said quietly. 'With a passion like that you must inspire your patients to get completely invested in their recovery.'

Abby shrugged off the compliment. 'I've heard a few good things about your work, too,' she said. 'It was fascinating to watch the microsurgery today. I hope I get a chance to work with him down the track.'

'He will need to start some gentle therapy in the next day or two,' Noah said. 'We'll be having a team meeting that will include your clinical director on Monday morning. Perhaps you can get involved right from day one?'

'I don't get to choose my patients but I'll keep my fingers crossed.' And not just because it would be such an interesting case, Abby thought. It would also mean that she would be working on the same team as Noah and it would be an opportunity to learn so much. She was smiling as she spoke but

Noah didn't notice. He was looking at his watch.

'And, with that reminder, I really need to head back. I said I'd be up on the ward later this evening to check on his post-op progress.' Noah got up from the table. 'Thank you so much, Hugh, for the invitation and to you as well, Lisa. I'm sure you were looking forward to coming home for a quiet evening that didn't include entertaining new colleagues.' His smile was warm. 'How long till the baby arrives?'

'A bit over a month,' Lisa told him. 'I'm not stopping work until I have to, though.'

'How exciting.' But Noah's tone didn't match his words and he was already turning away with no more than a nod in Abby's direction. 'I'm sure we'll meet again soon, Abby. Have a great weekend.'

Hugh went with Noah to the front door. Lisa and Abby exchanged a look.

'What was that about?' Lisa murmured. 'He seemed to be having a great time and then suddenly he couldn't wait to get away.'

'Guess he was thinking about his patient and that put him back into a professional zone.'

'Who's in a professional zone?' Hugh was walking back into the kitchen.

'Noah. He just switched off. As though he'd had more than enough of our company.'

'Ah…' Hugh sat back down at the table. 'I was surprised that he accepted my invitation to have a drink, to be honest, after I'd heard the gossip.'

'What gossip?'

'I went up to the ward before heading home, to see how the surgery had gone on Steve—the guy with the hand injury. I was in the corridor, trying to find his notes in the trolley, and I could hear the nurses in the office, chatting. And, yeah… I don't usually take any notice of that kind of stuff but…' Hugh sighed. 'It was why I invited him home for a beer. I thought he could use a friend.'

Abby was hanging onto every word Hugh was saying, her curiosity so sharp it felt like a door was being slammed in her face when he stopped speaking.

'And?' she demanded. 'You can't stop there…'

'I don't like gossip. Even if the story's true.'

'What story?' Lisa was as interested as

Abby. 'Come on, hon. You can't not tell us. Abby's going to be working with the man.' Her gaze slid sideways. 'I even got the impression that they might quite like each other now that they've got over the fact that Noah crashed into her car.'

But Hugh was shaking his head. 'That's just it. One of those nurses was saying how cute she thought the new surgeon was and the other one said she'd worked with him up north and there was no point in thinking that something might happen even if he *was* single.'

'Why not?' Abby asked.

'He's gay?' Lisa suggested.

Hugh shook his head. 'His wife died a few years ago. Some tragic accident, like a fall down some steps, with a head injury that was so catastrophic she was in cardiac arrest by the time she arrived in the ED. Love of his life, apparently.'

'Oh, no…that's tragic.'

'That wasn't even the worst of it. She was pregnant. Far enough along for them to do a post-mortem Caesarean in Emergency. The baby only lived for a day or two.'

Abby and Lisa exchanged another glance.

No wonder Noah hadn't seemed that interested in Lisa's pregnancy. Abby was actually finding it hard to take a breath because her throat had tightened up and there seemed to be something so heavy pressing on her chest that she put her hand there to see what it was.

'Anyway…he threw himself into his work and that was it. His personal life was out of bounds and he never socialised with anyone. So…' Hugh reached out to touch Lisa's hand as he smiled at her. 'I'm glad he agreed to come home for a drink. And I think you're right. He does like our Abby and why wouldn't he? They both share the same passion for the same kind of work.'

It was true. That shared passion had given them a genuine moment of connection. But maybe they had something else in common as well, Abby thought, and that was a handicap that affected every aspect of their lives. Hers might be very obvious but being in a wheelchair was only the external aspect of the challenges she faced. Noah's handicap was completely invisible because it was purely emotional but Abby was very well aware of how crippling that could be and her heart was breaking more than a little bit for him.

She'd always had the unwavering support of her sister to face all the hard stuff in her life but who did Noah have? Especially now that he'd moved to a new area and a new place of work. Did he want real friends in his life or were other people always required to stay within the boundaries of a professional relationship? And… Abby released the breath she'd finally managed to take in a long, slow sigh.

Even if he did have family or friends in his life and thought that was all he wanted to have, was he still lonely sometimes for something more?

Like she was?

CHAPTER THREE

THERE WAS A heavy silence in the room.

The four people behind this closed door were all aware of how serious this discussion was going to be. The man in the bed, with his injured hand elevated in a sling. His wife, sitting on his other side, holding his uninjured hand between both of hers. The surgeon who was in charge of his treatment. And… Abby.

'I've brought Abby along with me to talk to you today, Steve,' Noah told their patient. 'I know she started working with you after your first surgery and has been hoping— like we all have—that the second surgery on your thumb would restore an adequate blood supply.'

Steve nodded slowly but he managed a smile for Abby. They'd got on well from the first, very gentle passive therapy that she had begun with him.

'*Looks like you've faced a few challenges yourself,*' he'd told her. '*I'll bet you're the best person around for this job.*'

But it was Abby who'd been the first to notice the signs that the second surgery had failed. That the discoloration in Steve's thumb was the first indication of tissue death, nearly two weeks after the day she'd observed his initial surgery. The same day that she'd found out that she'd met Noah Baxter before. She had her suspicions that their new hand surgeon had something to do with her being assigned to Steve as his therapist but that only made her more determined to do the best job she could. It was very disappointing that they'd reached this point.

'As you know, your fingers are healing very well,' Noah continued. 'We did our best to restore an adequate blood supply to your thumb but I'm very sorry to say that it hasn't worked well enough.'

'But you can do another operation?' Pauline's tone was tentative. 'And fix it?'

It was no wonder that she was looking more and more tired, Abby thought, what with having to juggle babysitting or manage the travelling across the city with three children under five in order to make her daily hospital visits. Abby's relationship with her patient and his wife was still new but she could see that the recent extensive tests and this extra consultation had clearly raised stress levels considerably for both Pauline and Steve and her heart went out to the young couple.

'An adequate blood supply is vital to any part of the body,' Noah said. 'The blood carries oxygen and nutrients and antibodies to fight off infection. Without it, the cells can't survive and the tissue starts to die. That's what is happening with your thumb, Steve, and why those colour changes are happening.'

Even though it was only a couple of days since Abby had noticed the change and her alert had led to a barrage of tests for Steve, the tip of his thumb was already such a dark shade of red/brown that it was almost black.

'The risk of leaving dead tissue attached is that it can get infected and, if that infection travels to the rest of the body, it can cause sepsis, which can be very serious.'

'So I'm going to lose my thumb, then.' Steve's voice was wooden. 'And that means I'll never work again.'

'Oh, that's not true,' Pauline said quickly. 'There are lots of jobs that don't mean you have to use your hands so much.'

'Not the kind of job I love,' Steve said quietly. '*My* job. Where I get to work with my hands—growing stuff. With the best crowd of mates I've ever known... I'd go mad if I had to work in an office or a warehouse or something.'

Abby had heard a lot about Steve's work in the last couple of weeks. He worked at a hydroponic farm where they grew salad vegetables like lettuce and tomatoes and cucumbers. He mostly worked with the propagation and harvesting of the plants in the greenhouses. He'd just been helping out in the packing department for a morning when he'd had his horrible accident with the machinery. She also knew that Pauline had given up her part-time work after the arrival of their third baby and that things were financially tight.

'You are going to lose *this* thumb,' Noah confirmed. 'But it doesn't have to mean that you don't have *a* thumb.'

Both Steve and Pauline looked bewildered. Noah glanced at Abby and she could read the invitation to contribute to this discussion as clearly as if he'd spoken aloud. They'd only been working together for a couple of weeks with limited contact away from anything professional but, already, Abby was getting used to this ability of his to communicate silently.

It had been there from pretty much the first moment she'd met him, she realised. From when she'd seen the understanding that she'd been making a joke about never being able to walk again flash across his face. When she'd seen the appreciation in his eyes of her attempting humour in what could easily have escalated into a more stressful situation. When she'd heard him laugh…

'I think Mr Baxter asked me to come with him to talk to you today because I've had experience of working with a case like this,' she said. 'My patient was a lot further into his rehabilitation when I started working with him because he'd had his surgery and early rehab in another hospital, but he'd lost his thumb in a farming accident after getting caught up in rope when he was trying to deal with a stroppy bull. He was already back at work when I met him and he was really proud of what he could do again. He told me he'd been freaked out at the idea of his new thumb at first but it was the best thing he ever did.'

Abby opened a folder she had on her lap and took out a photograph. 'This is a picture of his thumb, six months after his transplant.'

'Oh, no…' Pauline looked horrified. 'He got someone else's thumb? Like a kidney transplant?'

'No. Look…' Abby showed them another photo, this one of both the man's hands side by side. 'Can you see a difference?'

'The thumb with the scar is a bit fatter,' Steve said. 'And the nail looks different.'

'It was his big toe,' Abby told them. 'That's where it was transplanted from. Actually, "transferred" is a better word to use.'

'It's a surgery that's been around for a surprisingly long time,' Noah added. 'But our techniques are improving all the time and the results can be very, very good.'

'But what does his foot look like?' Steve shook his head. 'I don't like this. My feet are important too. I'm on them all day. I want to be able to play footie with my boy down the track. Or take my family for a walk on the beach.'

'With therapy and gait training, you won't be disabled at all,' Abby assured him. She wanted to tell him just how much more important hands were than feet but she restricted herself to a smile. Steve had, after all, considered the fact that she was in a wheelchair as a point in her favour as his therapist.

'The left foot is usually the best choice,' Noah put in. 'Simply because you can lose a bit of push power without the big toe, and that means, with an automatic car, your driving isn't affected—by having to jump on the brake unexpectedly, for example.'

It was just a flash of a glance at Abby but she knew he was thinking of a moment when he'd needed to jump on his brake—in that split second before he'd bumped into the back of her car. Which meant he was thinking of her as a person, not simply as a colleague, and that gave her a frisson of something that had nothing at all to do with this patient.

As she laid out more photos for Steve and

Pauline to look at and Noah explained the procedure and the option of using a second toe instead of the big toe, along with the pros and cons, Abby found herself remembering that moment herself. And feeling curiously happy that it had happened.

Okay…that crush—and the ensuing disappointment that he hadn't called her—had been a bit silly but she was over that now. Meeting him properly and learning about the tragedy of him losing his wife and baby had put Abby in a very different space.

A safe space.

Because she didn't have to think about things that she'd avoided thinking about for such a long time.

Like sex…

Like how hard it might be for her to face—and overcome—a barrier that had been in place for several years now so that there was actually the possibility of a sexual encounter.

And, if she got that far, would she then have to worry about how different—and possibly disappointing—it might be for someone who was used to being with able-bodied women to be with someone whose legs looked so different? Who couldn't move in the same way? Who could, in fact, be far too passive for it to be a remotely exciting or satisfying experience?

It was better this way. To have a professional relationship with someone who could teach her so much. And to develop a friendship where they could both relax and enjoy each other's company. Where they could make each other laugh. It might, in fact, be enough for her to get past the barrier that had pretty much stopped her forming a meaningful relationship with any man. The subtle nod of Abby's head might have been an agreement with herself but it looked as though she was agreeing with what Noah was saying now.

'So, using the second toe means less deformity on the foot, but the big toe will look so much more like a thumb—as you can see from the photos that Abby's shown you.'

'What about the surgery?' Pauline asked. 'Would you do the transplant at the same time as taking off the thumb or does that have to heal first?'

'It's better to do the transfer at the same time than delay. That way we can be sure we're matching things up as well as possible and can attach nerves and blood vessels more accurately. The surgery itself is long. It could take between eight and twelve hours.'

'The rehab is long, too,' Abby warned. 'To get a good result you have to be willing to face some pretty rigorous and time-consuming therapy. There's six weeks to allow for bones to heal. We'll be doing therapy during that period, of course, to keep everything mobile, but the really intense work will start after that.'

'How long did it take for that chap?' Steve pointed at the first photo Abby had shown them. Till he got back to his work on the farm?'

'Six months,' she told him. 'And he had really good sensation in his thumb and enough range of movement and strength to do most of the things he needed to do in his job.'

Steve closed his eyes and lay back against his pillow. 'I dunno,' he muttered. 'It just seems…really weird. It's doing my head in.'

'I understand.' Noah got to his feet. 'We'll leave you to think about it. Maybe write down any worries or questions you might come up with and we'll talk again later. I'll come and see you tomorrow morning before my ward round. Or you can page me anytime and I'll come as soon as I'm free.'

'I'll be available too,' Abby promised. 'Though I'm sure Mr Baxter will be able to answer a lot more questions than I can.'

She could feel Steve watching he as she turned her chair and headed for the door. Could he see how important her thumb was, perhaps?

Maybe Noah was watching her as well and thinking along the same lines.

'Keep in mind that the thumb is the most debilitating digit to lose as far as hand function is concerned,' he said quietly. 'And that the benefits of a toe transfer far outweigh the risks.'

Noah walked with Abby as she headed back to her office.

'I've got an outpatient clinic starting in fifteen minutes,' he said. 'Maybe I can scrounge a cup of coffee in your staffroom?'

'Of course. You're as much a part of the staff of the hand clinic as anyone else.'

She showed him where to find the mugs and the biscuit tin when they arrived back in her small corner of this large hospital. 'Do you think Steve will agree to the surgery?'

'I hope so.' Noah sat down on one of the armchairs in the room. 'It can take a bit of time to get your head around the concept, though.' He shifted a bag on the low table between chairs to have a space to put his mug.

'Oh…that's mine,' Abby said. 'I wondered where that had got to.'

He handed her the bag, frowning as the blunt point of a thick needle pierced the plastic.

'I'm learning to knit,' Abby explained. 'And it's harder than it looks. I suspect I left it in here and forgot about it on purpose.'

Noah was grinning at her.

'What's funny?'

'The idea of you knitting,' he said.

'I'm about to become an aunty. I thought maybe I should learn how to make a pair of booties or something. I know…' she made a face. 'It's not really me, is it? I know it's got trendy but I still feel like I'm doing old-lady stuff.'

'It does seem about as likely as… I don't know…me playing wheelchair basketball.'

'That wouldn't be a strange thing to do. You'd love it.'

'But I'm not in a wheelchair.'

'You don't have to be, apart from when you're playing. Able-bodied people are allowed.'

'Really?'

'Why not?' Abby shrugged. 'The wheelchair is just a tool. Like using ice skates or a bicycle or something.'

'But it doesn't seem fair. Don't able-bodied people have an advantage?'

Abby smiled. 'No. They just think they do—until they have a go. The only difference is that they have higher points.' It was time she went back to her office and reviewed patient files for the people she would be working with for the rest of the day but stealing a few minutes to keep talking to Noah was irresistible.

'Players get classified according to their level of disability,' she explained. 'The total number of points allowed on the court at any time, adding up the five players, is fourteen. It's all about control of trunk movement. If you have little or no control, you score one point zero. If you have complete control in all directions, you score four point five. As an able-bodied person, you'd score four point five.'

'How much do you score?'

'I'm a four point five, too,' Abby told him. 'My spinal injury was low lumbar so I'm really very lucky. I even got to avoid the total lack of bladder and bowel control that most paraplegics have to deal with.' She bit her lip at the expression on Noah's face. 'Sorry…too much information?'

'No…not at all.' Noah was smiling now. 'I was just thinking that I might like to try the basketball—especially in weather like this when it's too wet to be pleasant getting out for a run. If you didn't set out to wipe the floor with me, that is.'

'Come along, then.' The idea that Noah might want to join in the sport she loved so much was making Abby feel astonishingly happy. 'Tomorrow's a training session and newbies are always welcome. It's friendly and relaxed. I'll send you the address for the gym and you can use one of the extra sports chairs that are stored there.'

'You said this would be relaxing.' Noah could feel his soaked shirt sticking to his back and he knew the muscles in his arms were going to be complaining tomorrow.

'I said relaxed, not relax*ing*.' Abby was waiting for the moment he lost control of the ball as he tried to bounce it and move his chair at the same time. She swooped as soon as he did and then she was off, showing him how it was done as she rolled almost the full length of the court before taking aim and scoring a goal.

He could use both hands to propel the chair now and the physical effort was actually very welcome. This was far more interesting than simply going for a run because he needed to use his brain as well as his body. The effort involved was also exactly what he'd needed after a frustrating end to his day. Steve had decided against the toe transfer and wasn't ready to sign a consent form for an amputation either. He was upset and miserable and refusing to talk to anyone, including his wife. When Abby had arrived for his therapy session she'd been told, very rudely, to "get lost".

Not that she'd taken it personally. 'I'll try again tomorrow,' she'd told Noah. 'We'll win in the end, you'll see. I'm going to have a quiet word with Pauline and see if we can work together to persuade him that it's the best thing to do.

He was feeling a lot more optimistic himself now, as if Abby's determination and confidence was contagious. Although she'd just demonstrated that she was far more capable than him, she hadn't wiped the floor with him as he'd had his first go at her sport. Like her teammates, she'd been patient. And generous. And the amount of laughter on court had been even more contagious.

Noah hadn't felt this good in what felt like for ever. He knew he was beaming as he finally unstrapped his legs and got out of the chair.

Abby rolled up beside him. 'What's the verdict?'

'Great exercise, in good company, with so much fun thrown in? What's not to love?'

'This weather?' Abby had to raise her voice to be heard over the sudden drumming of hail on the roof of the gymnasium. A crack of thunder a few seconds later made her groan. 'I hope it stops before we get to the car park. It's times like this I'm envious of people who get to hold an umbrella and run and jump into their cars as fast as possible.'

'I've got a massive umbrella in my car. If it's still raining, I can help—with the chair or something?'

The offer was matter-of-fact and wasn't making any assumptions about what Abby was, or was not, capable of managing for herself. It reminded Abby of their first meeting. That, while he might recognise that something was more difficult for her, he saw *her* before he saw a disabled woman.

'That would be great. It'll probably blow over by the time we're out of the showers but, in the time-honoured tradition of welcoming newbies, I'd be happy to shout you a beer in the local pub.'

The storm hadn't blown over by the time Abby found Noah waiting for her by the main doors of the gym. If anything, it was worse. His umbrella was threatening to blow inside out and she barely heard her phone ringing over the noise of the heavy rain. She stayed under the shelter of the foyer to answer the call when she saw it was her brother-in-law's number. Hugh might talk to her on Lisa's phone but he never called himself. The beat of alarm intensified when she heard a voice she didn't recognise on the other end of the line.

'Who is this?' Abby demanded. 'And why have you got Hugh's phone?'

Noah's glance was sharp. Nobody could have missed the level of anxiety in her tone.

'I'm Greg, one of the consultants in ED. Hugh threw his phone to me and asked me to call. He's just rushed upstairs to Maternity with Lisa.'

'Oh, my God…what's happened? Is she okay? Is the baby okay?'

'They're fine. The baby's just decided to arrive early, that's all. In fact, it might have been born in the lift. Lisa was asking for you…'

'Oh…no… If you can, tell her I'm on my way.' Abby didn't wait for Noah to hold his umbrella over her as she propelled herself outside. 'It's Lisa,' she called over her shoulder. 'She's in labour. I've got to get to the hospital.'

'What about your other chair?' Noah was struggling to keep his umbrella the right way out as he caught up with her.

'Coach will sort it. There's plenty of room

for storage.' Abby's car was in one of the
first parking spaces but, as she approached,
her heart sank like a stone.

'*No*…not now. *Please*…not now…'

Her rear tyre was as flat as a pancake.
Noah had the umbrella over her head but
enough rain was being blown sideways to
feel miserably cold. For one horrible, scary
moment Abby had no idea what to do. Noah,
however, was completely calm.

'My SUV,' he said. 'You won't even need
to fold up your chair. It'll fit into the back,
no problem. We'll sort your car later.'

The only relief that could be bigger than
not having to think of a way out of this problem would be to know that both Lisa and the
baby were fine. Abby was more than happy
to let Noah take charge. She transferred herself into his passenger seat with a bit of extra
effort because it was higher than the seats
in her car and strapped herself in as Noah
stowed the chair in the back. He drove as
swiftly as the appalling conditions allowed
and then they reversed the procedure and
made a dash from the parking building to
the hospital entrance. Even well inside the
huge building, they could still hear the crack

of fresh thunder as they reached the bank of elevators. There was certainly no missing the way the lights flickered, went out completely and then came back on.

They flickered again as Abby pushed the button for the second floor where Maternity was located and Noah frowned.

'Might not be safe to use these,' he said.

'Isn't there an emergency generator that comes on if there's a power outage?'

'Yes, but it's prioritised to cover critical areas first, like Theatres and ICU. Might take a while to get to a lift.'

As if to add weight to his warning, the lights flickered again. A security guard was coming down the corridor towards the emergency department.

'Don't use the lifts,' he told them. 'We don't want anyone trapped if the power goes out completely.'

Abby shook her head. This couldn't be happening. His sister was two floors above them and there was no way she could get any closer without using a lift because the only other way up was the stairwell on the far side of the elevators.

Noah had followed her despairing glance.

Then he caught Abby's gaze and it was another one of those silent, fast-as-light exchanges.

I could carry you up the stairs. Is it that important to get there fast?

Yes...it's the only thing that's important right now...

The offer had been impulsive.

Done without thinking about any potential consequences but it was the right thing to do and Noah wasn't about to second-guess the plan. He called to the security guard, who turned back.

'Could you find a safe space for a wheelchair for a while? We need to use the stairs.'

'No worries, mate. I'll put it in ED Reception.'

He waited while Noah lifted Abby from the chair into his arms and then whisked the chair away. There was certainly no turning back now, although it felt awkward as he bumped the firestop door open with his back and then faced the staircase.

'You might regret this.' Abby's voice sounded as if it was hard to keep her tone light. 'I'm not exactly a featherweight.'

It wasn't the weight of Abby in his arms that might make Noah regret his offer. It was far more likely to be the feel of holding a woman this close because…because the last woman he'd held like this had been his wife, Ellen. But it was okay, because this was an emergency and all he had to do was get her to Maternity and then find out where her sister was, and the physical effort, on top of what he'd already done this evening, was enough to drive anything else from his awareness.

Like the way her arms were wrapped around his neck, holding on for dear life, and the softness of her breast pressing against his arm. Or that smell of…what was it…something like apple blossom? It had to be her shampoo or soap. Surely nobody's skin could smell that good naturally?

There was a nurse near the labour ward's reception desk. 'Abby? We were told to look out for you. Come with me…' She took off, without giving Noah the chance to ask if they might have a wheelchair available. He couldn't exactly slow down and look for one himself either, which meant that when they got to the room Lisa was in, there was nothing for it but to carry Abby inside. Which also meant that Noah was suddenly in a space he really didn't want to be in—with a young mother sitting on a bed, her husband perched beside her with his arm around her shoulders, looking down to where she was cradling their newborn child in her arms.

He could actually feel the emotion that was taking over Abby. The tension that was exploding into something else. That kind of wonder and joy that had been almost missing for him when he'd first seen his child because he'd been inside such a dark cloud of horror at the same time. He'd felt flashes of it, however. Enough to recognise that Abby was overwhelmed by it now. Enough to know that he didn't want to be dragged back into his own past like this.

Gently, he put Abby down into the armchair in the room and stepped back, ready to excuse himself and let the family have this special time together. He wasn't needed any more. Hugh could sort out getting Abby's chair back and helping to deal with the flat tyre on her car.

But Lisa wanted to thank him for making sure that Abby had got here. And Hugh was taking the tiny bundle out of Lisa's arms and was giving it to Abby and…the expression on her face was…well, it was so raw and so powerful that the breath caught in his throat. Noah could actually feel his throat tightening so much it was painful and there was a sting at the back of his eyes that he recognised from long ago.

He had to get out. Now. Before he could get sucked into that feeling of loss. Of being confronted with something he'd wanted so much but could now never have. A family of his own. He was aware of something else as well. He could see—and feel—the love between the people in this room and, right now, especially between Abby and the tiny person she was holding in her arms like the most precious thing to ever exist. A collage of at least a dozen thoughts flashed through his head in the fraction of time it took for him to smile and turn away.

Meeting Abby Phillips and the way she'd made him laugh. Seeing her hair lit up like a halo that day when she had been sitting in the gallery above his operating theatre. That she had known his favourite quote and spoken it with him with such feeling. The fierce determination that was obvious so often but really unleashed on a basketball court but the way it was tempered by generosity and patience.

She was an astonishing person and, in this heart-melting moment, Noah's only—and fervent—wish was that Abby would never have to suffer the heartbreak of losing someone precious to her, like her sister or that brand-new baby, because she deserved so much more than that. She deserved every happiness that life could possibly provide, in fact.

CHAPTER FOUR

'Hey…guess what?'

Abby looked up to see Noah poking his head around the door of the treatment room. Her patient, sitting beside her at the table, was still staring at her hand as if willing it to move. Abby nodded and put up her index finger, signalling to Noah that she would be able to talk to him in a minute.

'Try this one, again, Audrey. Relax your fingers and thumb and make an "O" by touching your thumb to your index finger. Straighten your fingers and then touch your middle finger. Straighten again and repeat for each finger. I'll be back in a sec.'

Turning her chair, she rolled towards Noah, happy to interrupt this session with a patient because it was almost finished anyway but more, because she hadn't seen him for a couple of days—ever since her niece had arrived so unexpectedly on that stormy night—so she hadn't had the chance to thank him for his help.

The night was a bit of blur, to be honest, but there were two memories that stood out. One was the feeling of holding that tiny baby in her arms, the astonishing amount of love she could feel for someone she was meeting for the very first time, and the total conviction that to become a mother was most definitely something she wanted in her own future. The other memory…well, that was the way she'd felt when *she* had been held in someone else's arms. Noah's, to be precise.

She'd been held in the arms of a countless number of people in her lifetime. Not so much these days, of course, but it did happen occasionally—like when Alex, the orthopaedic registrar, had helped her negotiate the tricky access to the operating theatre gallery. Noah had only been offering the same kind of assistance and, while it had actually been happening, Abby had been too stressed about seeing her sister to acknowledge how different it had been.

It was only much, much later, when all the

drama of that night had settled down and her flat tyre had been taken care of by a car rescue service and she had been back home and safe in her own bed that she'd realised just how strong that memory was. If she thought about it, she could still feel the strength that had been in his arms, despite the workout he'd just given them on the basketball court. She could feel his muscles working beneath where she'd been hanging onto his neck and she could smell his warmth and that masculine undertone that could have been the lingering scent of an aftershave but which she suspected was purely his own. She had also felt the tension when he'd carried her into Lisa's room and she'd known why when she'd seen the expression on his face just before he'd escaped.

Okay…make that three memories because she wasn't about to forget that haunted look on Noah's face as he'd left Lisa's room in the maternity ward. How hard had it been for him to carry her into that room when it had to have triggered memories of a very different birth of a baby? No wonder he'd been avoiding her for the last couple of days and pulling the mantle of his professional life around him like a protective cloak. Interrupting a therapy session wasn't the most professional thing to do, mind you, and Noah wasn't looking at all haunted now. He was, in fact, looking almost as happy as he had when he'd come off the basketball court the other night.

'He said *yes*.'

Abby grinned back. 'The last time someone told me that and was looking this happy was when a friend came into my room at my uni hostel in the middle of the night to tell me about proposing to her boyfriend.'

Noah blinked and Abby had to give herself a mental shake. What a stupid thing to say. Noah probably wanted to avoid memories of proposals and marriages about as much as being close to newborn babies.

But he was still smiling. 'Steve,' he added. He was holding a clipboard in his hand that had papers attached to it. 'He's signed all the consent forms. I thought you might like to come to the team meeting later this afternoon when we start planning the surgery.'

'Oh…that's wonderful news. I'll start making my own treatment plans for after the surgery. If I'm still going to be his therapist?'

his own investment in the upcoming surgery for Steve. This was going to be a very long and technically demanding procedure but it was an intriguing solution to a major issue and everybody here knew what a huge difference it could make, not only to a young father but for his whole family.

As Noah clicked through and discussed slides that labelled the tendons, nerves and blood vessels that would need to be dissected free of the foot and left attached to the isolated toe for the implant surgery, he could feel a faint echo of what he'd said about Steve sitting there in the back of his mind. It was quite astonishing, in fact, that he could be giving a seamless presentation like this and that part of his brain could be aware of something that had nothing to do with anatomy or surgical procedures or anything to do with his patient at all, really. Except it did, didn't it? It was the core of the reason they were all here and why they were so passionate about their work.

It was that notion of family, that's what it was.

Noah wasn't consciously thinking about it, of course, but he could feel it—like a vast

'As a matter of fact, he said that was part of the deal.' There were crinkles at the corners of Noah's eyes, even though his smile was fading. 'He said that was what had changed his mind was the conversation he'd had with you and Pauline this morning. About…babies?'

Abby's smile was a bit misty. 'I was telling him about the excitement of the other night. About how amazing it was to be holding a brand-new baby. And Pauline was helping Steve to hold *his* baby and we reminded him of all the things he'd be able to do with her more easily if he had a new thumb. Like giving her a bath or holding her hand to walk her to school or…' Abby's voice trailed away. Was she rubbing salt into a wound that Noah was always going to have, by reminding him of his own loss? He didn't seem upset, though, even though that smile had vanished.

'Five o'clock, then? In the conference room?'

'I'll be there.' She still hadn't had the chance to thank Noah for his help the other night but this wasn't the time either. He was already disappearing through the door and, behind her, Audrey was sounding frustrated.

'As a matter of fact, he said that was part of the deal.' There were crinkles at the corners of Noah's eyes, even though his smile was fading. 'He said that was what had changed his mind was the conversation he'd had with you and Pauline this morning. About…babies?'

Abby's smile was a bit misty. 'I was telling him about the excitement of the other night. About how amazing it was to be holding a brand-new baby. And Pauline was helping Steve to hold *his* baby and we reminded him of all the things he'd be able to do with her more easily if he had a new thumb. Like giving her a bath or holding her hand to walk her to school or…' Abby's voice trailed away. Was she rubbing salt into a wound that Noah was always going to have, by reminding him of his own loss? He didn't seem upset, though, even though that smile had vanished.

'Five o'clock, then? In the conference room?'

'I'll be there.' She still hadn't had the chance to thank Noah for his help the other night but this wasn't the time either. He was already disappearing through the door and, behind her, Audrey was sounding frustrated.

'I can't do it. I can't make my thumb touch my ring finger and it's miles away from my pinkie.'

Abby turned back to her patient. 'It'll come, don't worry. Just think about how far you've come since the cast came off your wrist. This is something you can practise at home and every time you do it, you'll be getting a little closer to making it happen. Now…let's try something else…'

Places at the long, oval table in the conference room were full by the time Noah had hooked his laptop up to the data projector ready for his presentation. He turned to the group and their conversations faded instantly. For many of the people here—the same mix of surgeons and senior ancillary staff that had been involved in Steve's earlier surgeries—the procedure he was about to discuss would be a first and there was a distinct air of professional interest in the room. A hum of excitement, even, and he could feel the intensity of their focus on him. Especially Abby's…

'So…big toe transplantation has proven itself to be the ideal form of thumb reconstruction in the case of traumatic thumb loss,' he began. 'It has a single interphalangeal joint just like the thumb and, for most people, the length and appearance of the big toe is not dissimilar to their other thumb.'

The photograph he put up was the one that he and Abby had shown Steve when they'd been telling him about the option of this surgery and that felt a lot longer ago than a couple of days. It wasn't so much that so many things had happened but that they'd dragged him back to such a traumatic episode of his personal history. Why was it that the time period to deal with difficult things seemed to stretch out but the most enjoyable things went past in a flash—like that first attempt he'd made at playing wheelchair basketball?

'As you all know,' he continued, 'Steve is a father to three children, the youngest of whom is just a baby. He's fortunate enough to have a strong and supportive marriage, he has many years ahead of him to provide for his family and he's extremely motivated to work hard towards a successful outcome and, preferably, to return to a job he loves that requires a good level of hand function.'

He could feel a reflection in the room of

his own investment in the upcoming surgery for Steve. This was going to be a very long and technically demanding procedure but it was an intriguing solution to a major issue and everybody here knew what a huge difference it could make, not only to a young father but for his whole family.

As Noah clicked through and discussed slides that labelled the tendons, nerves and blood vessels that would need to be dissected free of the foot and left attached to the isolated toe for the implant surgery, he could feel a faint echo of what he'd said about Steve sitting there in the back of his mind. It was quite astonishing, in fact, that he could be giving a seamless presentation like this and that part of his brain could be aware of something that had nothing to do with anatomy or surgical procedures or anything to do with his patient at all, really. Except it did, didn't it? It was the core of the reason they were all here and why they were so passionate about their work.

It was that notion of family, that's what it was.

Noah wasn't consciously thinking about it, of course, but he could feel it—like a vast space behind an open door. And that door was only open as far as it was because he'd had to confront his own loss of family all over again the other night, and he hadn't been prepared for that at all. He hadn't been prepared for that close physical contact when he'd been carrying Abby either—or the disturbing dreams it seemed to have triggered for the last couple of nights—but it had been the unexpected proximity to Lisa's baby in the first few minutes of its life that had really done his head in.

He pressed the arrow button on his keyboard to bring up a new diagram. A photograph this time of a foot with lines drawn on it with a marker pen. It took only a split second to push that button but it was long enough for one of those momentary flashbacks that he'd never been able to get away from, especially if he saw the tiny face of a newborn or heard that distinctive warbling cry. He'd got very good at pushing the flashbacks away, however, and, without missing a beat, Noah dealt with that image in his mind by flicking it away as if it were no more than an annoying fly near his face. How weird was it, though, that just a glimpse could still carry the weight of unbearable emotions that were associated with that image of Ellen, lying there on a bed in the emergency department.

The consultant in charge of her attempted resuscitation was looking up at the clock to record the time of death. The looks that were exchanged amongst the crowd of people in the room were acknowledging that they'd failed but also that there were two patients involved here. The decision to do something that was too horrific to even contemplate— a post-mortem Caesarean—was being made in that instant and Noah could only grapple with the way his heart was being so completely torn between grief and hope as he saw that tiny baby coming into the world and struggling to take her first breaths.

And then…as they always did—the unwanted images and echoes of associated feelings vanished and it had all happened so fast that nobody would ever guess they'd been there. Except… Noah looked up as he took a breath to talk about this new photograph. His gaze happened to catch Abby's and he had the oddest sensation—like the softest touch on the back of his neck—that made him wonder if she might see more than he realised.

'These lines are the markers for the initial incision,' he said, turning back to point to the screen. 'As you can see, it extends well in to the first web space. We need to leave sufficient flap length to let us close up with minimal shortening of the first metatarsal. These next photos will demonstrate the dissection that needs to happen to identify the arterial branches, the extensor tendon and a dorsal vein...'

There would be two teams working in Theatre, one to harvest the toe and then repair the foot and the other to prepare the site on the hand and then do the implantation.

'When the implantation team is ready, that's when we ligate and transect the dominant artery and vein on the toe. The sequence for implantation is, as you'd expect—bone, extensor tendon, flexor tendon, nerves, artery, vein and finally the skin.'

Noah flipped through slide after slide that covered the rest of this surgery and answered any queries that the team came up with. One of the last was from an ICU consultant.

'How long do you expect he'll need to be in the unit?'

'Three to five days. We'll need to keep a close eye on limb baselines with the help of a Doppler signal and continuous pulse oximetry. It's going to take a few days at least to get all our ducks in a row for a major surgery like this so we've got plenty of time to meet and put a more extensive plan in place. I'll try and get to everyone involved so that we can discuss any details that this overview might have missed.'

There were nods around the table and people began gathering any personal items like notepads and phones. This meeting was almost over.

'Just to finish up,' Noah continued, 'I'd like to—belatedly—welcome Abby Phillips to this meeting. Rehabilitation in a case like this is of huge importance if we're going to get a successful outcome. Do you have any comments you'd like to make, Abby? Or questions to ask?'

'I understand that gentle mobilisation can start as early as three to four days after the procedure if the bone fixation is stable and that starting active exercises will depend on the strength of the tendon repairs. The real work of strengthening and vocational therapy will start at about the two-month mark, yes?'

Noah nodded. 'Let's sort out a time for us to meet before you head away. Same goes for everybody else—I've got my diary here. Thank you for taking the time to come to this meeting and I look forward to working with you all again.'

Abby seemed perfectly happy to wait while he made arrangements to talk through the case in more detail with the various specialists involved and, for his part, Noah felt curiously happy that she was here and waiting for him. He was getting to know his new colleagues now and they were great people to be working with but Abby definitely stood out from the rest of them. She stood out from everyone he'd ever met in his life, to be honest.

He'd never met anyone who used humour the way she automatically did to diffuse any potential tense moment. She'd done that within minutes of meeting him, joking that she might never walk again after that accident, and she'd done it again today, when she'd told him he was repeating the words of someone who'd just proposed to their boyfriend. And she'd done that because she recognised that there was tension between them. Because he'd been avoiding her—avoiding anything other than purely work—after what had happened the other night.

Noah knew perfectly well that hospital grapevines worked between cities as much as departments. That everybody at St John's had probably heard about his tragic backstory within a very short time of him walking through the doors, and he was quite used to the occasional glance coming his way that varied from curious to being full of pity. It was rare to get one that made him feel that someone actually understood how hard it had been, however, especially when it could acknowledge a struggle with no hint of pity or OTT admiration, and he'd received a glance exactly like that in the last moment before he'd escaped Lisa's room in the maternity ward.

Abby had already got past his usual barrier that kept him from engaging in social events with the people he worked with by persuading him to go to that basketball training session but that hadn't been exactly social, had it? It had been exercise and stress relief and he'd been attracted to the idea because it was just so different from anything he'd ever done before. New ground—and new ground was the best because it was guaranteed not to trigger flashbacks of any kind.

Finally, they were the only two people left in the conference room and Noah found himself deliberately relaxing. There was a huge amount of preparation for the gruelling stint in Theatre that Steve's surgery would entail and, from experience, he knew that he needed to make the most of any downtime before that.

'How's your diary looking for meeting times?'

'A lot emptier than yours, I expect.' She was smiling at him. 'It's a big challenge, isn't it?'

'I love a challenge.' Noah was smiling back. 'I suspect you do as well.'

'Story of my life. I'd probably get bored in no time without one.' Abby's tone was light but there was something serious in her gaze. 'Having said that, though, there are the occasional challenges that can make me feel kind of vulnerable and I had one of those the other night—with that flat tyre and then the power cuts. I've been waiting for a chance to thank you for helping me.'

Noah tried to shrug off the thanks. Already, he was waiting for a flashback and preparing himself to find a distraction.

'And, what's more, you managed to do it without reminding me that I have limitations,' Abby added. 'There's not many people who can step in like that and let someone like me keep their dignity.'

Noah had found a new smile. 'I think you'd keep your dignity in any situation. From what I've seen, you own whatever you choose to tackle.'

It was Abby's turn to shrug something off. Maybe she didn't like compliments?

'Anyway… I was trying to think of a way to say thank you but, I dunno, I didn't think flowers or chocolates would cut the mustard.'

That made Noah's breath come out in a huff of laughter. 'Touché,' he murmured. 'We do have that in common, I guess.'

'So I came up with the idea of offering to

cook you dinner,' Abby continued. 'It's not common knowledge but one of my splinter skills is that I'm a fabulous cook. I've thought about entering one of the television chef competitions, in fact.'

'Oh?' Noah was impressed. Was there anything Abby wasn't good at? 'I can't cook to save myself. I usually end up getting those ready-made meals from the supermarket. Some of them are surprisingly good, mind you.'

Abby waved a hand dismissively. 'Can't compete with made from scratch. So, that's a yes, then? We could kill two birds with one stone and talk about Steve's rehab and that way you'll have more time in your schedule for any extra meetings you might need.'

'You mean tonight?'

Her glance held a glint of amusement this time. 'No time like the present. I often find if you give yourself too much time to think about something, you'll just come up with a whole bunch of reasons why it isn't a good idea. Unless you've got other plans?'

How did she know that he was already formulating a polite reason why he couldn't have dinner with her tonight? The same way she knew he didn't have anything on his agenda for the evening, other than to spend hours going over his plans for Steve's surgery? She probably knew why he would back away at the speed of light from a dinner invitation from a single woman, too, but that clearly wasn't going to be a barrier in a friendship that suddenly felt remarkably safe. Different.

New ground.

'No other plans,' he heard himself saying aloud. 'And a home-cooked meal does sound like a treat. Give me your address and a time and I'll be there.'

Abby hurriedly threw the packaging from the ready-made meals into her rubbish bin before speeding to her front door when the bell rang.

'I didn't realise you lived so close to the staff quarters,' Noah said. 'Walking distance.'

'It's a great location.' Abby nodded. 'But I just loved the building for its character. High ceilings like this give it such a feeling of spaciousness.'

So did having minimal furniture, of course,

polished wooden or tile floors throughout with no rugs to break the smooth surface, and wider than normal doors to accommodate her wheelchair.

'I love it.' Noah belatedly remembered that he had a bottle of wine tucked under his arm. 'Hope you like red?'

'It'll be perfect with our dinner but I have to say I'm a bubbles girl. Can I interest you in a glass of Prosecco to start with?'

Noah was smiling. 'Somehow that doesn't surprise me.'

'Sadly, I've developed a taste for French champagne.' Abby led the way past the doors leading to her bedroom and the bathroom, into the open-plan kitchen living area of her remodelled ground-floor apartment. Two couches marked off the corner where her gas fire flickered within its antique iron casing. A dining table and chairs separated that corner from the kitchen.

'And that's sad?'

'Only because it's out of my budget. I blame my sister, Lisa. And Hugh, of course. Remind me to tell you the story of how they got together sometime.'

'I'm guessing it involved French champagne?' But Noah wasn't waiting for confirmation. He was looking up at the ornate cornice of the plaster ceilings. 'This is amazing. You've got a chandelier even.'

'I have excellent taste,' Abby agreed. She opened the fridge and took out the chilled bottle of sparkling wine. 'I know it's a work night but we don't have to drink it all.'

'I make it a policy to find at least a bit of time to relax when I've got a big surgery coming up. If you don't charge your batteries beforehand it can be a struggle to stay focused for what could be a twelve-hour stint.'

'I'll bet.' Abby handed him the bottle. 'Could you do the honours? I'm just going to check on the oven.'

'Whatever it is smells delicious.'

'Beef Wellington,' Abby told him, relieved that she had a good reason not to be meeting his gaze. 'Just individual-sized ones.'

'I'm impressed.' Noah was eyeing the work surfaces of her kitchen now. 'If I tried to make something that complicated, my kitchen would be a complete bombsite.'

'Ah…' Hadn't Abby heard somewhere that if you wanted to make a lie convincing, the best thing to do was to add in at least an element of truth? 'Well, I have to admit, these were prepared earlier. I had them in the freezer for when I needed a nice meal in a hurry.'

The cork came out of the bottle with a pop and Noah poured the wine into the two glasses Abby provided. He scooped up the cork, wire and foil and headed for the rubbish bin before Abby could stop him but, to her relief, he didn't notice what she'd put in the bin only minutes ago. Even so, she decided it would be a good idea to distract him further.

'Let's sit at the table for now. I printed off a rough outline of a rehab plan for Steve before I left work.'

'Really? That was only an hour or so ago. You did a plan, came home, got changed and whipped up a gourmet dinner and you don't even look out of breath.' He held his glass up in a toast. 'Very impressive.'

'Hmm.' Was it her imagination or was there a note of amusement in his voice?

It was a bit distracting that he'd noticed she had changed her clothes as well. While favouring a more formal skirt and blouse under her white coat at work, Abby was always keen to get into her favourite leggings and a comfortable sweatshirt as soon as she got home. Was Noah feeling less comfortable because he'd noticed the difference? Or because he was in her home and not in an impersonal space like the gymnasium where they'd last met out of work hours? She could fix that. Abby pushed a thin sheaf of papers towards Noah.

'It's only a rough outline, so far,' she explained. 'I was focusing on the sensory rehabilitation because of how it can speed up the axonal regeneration.'

'That's true. And it's a critical element. Not just for repairing the axons but because it helps interpretation of the altered sensory impulses reaching the central nervous system.'

Yes—it seemed that a professional discussion was ironically exactly what Noah needed to relax out of work hours. Abby took a sip of her wine as she watched Noah begin to scan her pages. He had a few questions, some excellent suggestions and genuine praise for her outline.

'There's a great article I came across in a neurology journal recently about the sensory, emotional and cognitive factors and their interplay in the perception of pain. It was directly related to sensory rehabilitation. I could find it online for you if you like.'

'That would be awesome. But let's eat first. No...don't move,' Abby ordered. 'I'll get everything. I hope you're hungry.'

She ferried plates and cutlery to the table and the bowl of salad from the fridge. She handed Noah the bottle of red wine and a corkscrew before getting the food from the oven and transferring it to a pretty serving platter.

They ate in an appreciative silence to begin with.

'This is *so* good,' Noah finally said. 'Perfect.'

'I'm so glad you like it.'

'Love it.' Noah had almost finished the large puff-pastry square filled with beef, mushroom and chicken liver pâté. 'In fact, it's been one of my favourite meals from the gourmet section of the supermarket for a long time.'

Abby closed her eyes. 'Uh-oh,' she murmured. 'I'm busted, aren't I?'

'So busted,' Noah agreed. 'But they're a

great range of ready meals, aren't they? I rather like the cottage pie as well.'

'Oh, me too. And have you tried the chilli con carne?'

'Delicious. Not quite as good as the spaghetti carbonara, perhaps.'

They were both laughing by now.

'And there I was,' Noah said sadly, 'believing that you were some sort of domestic goddess and that you had splinter skills that I could never dream of competing with.'

Abby bit her lip. 'I did *think* of cooking something from scratch,' she said. 'But that would have been cruel. My splinter skill of cooking is on a par with my ability to knit.' She caught Noah's gaze, aiming for an apologetic glance but knowing she was finding this too funny to carry it off. 'But you wouldn't have come if I told you what a crap cook I was, would you? And I really did want to do something to say thanks.'

'It wasn't necessary,' Noah said. 'And I would have come even if it was just beans on toast. I like you, Abby Phillips.'

'I like you, too,' Abby responded lightly. 'And I'll be totally up front and confess that I also didn't make the salted caramel cheesecake ice cream I got for our dessert. Would you like to sit by the fire and relax with it?'

'Sounds perfect. Why don't we have some more of those bubbles with it as well? It's not as if I have to drive home.'

'And I don't even have to walk home.' Abby grinned. 'I like the way you think, Mr Baxter.'

Like…it was the second time she'd used that insipid little word in less than a minute. As she got the ice cream from the freezer and pulled bowls from a cupboard, Abby could see Noah walking towards the other side of this big room to put the Prosecco and glasses on one of the low tables beside the couches.

He looked right at home here, with his height not at all out of place beneath her high ceilings. At home and relaxed and…just as gorgeous as she'd remembered him being when she'd allowed herself to play with the delicious fantasies that her initial crush had created.

Which had been all very well when they were just that—fantasies. How much of a relief had it been, though, to discover that Noah wasn't ever going to want to be more than a friend? To back off from having to confront an anxiety that had been buried for years? Those deep, dark doubts about whether someone would find her as attractive as someone able-bodied and, worse, whether that fear of being unable to protect herself enough might resurface and make it impossible for her to go that far?

It had still been easy, despite having Noah in her own home, thanks to the formality of being at a table and the professional element that talking about Steve's upcoming surgery and rehabilitation had provided. But this… transferring herself from her wheelchair to one of the squashy, feather-filled pillows of her couch, in front of a flickering fire, with not only a bowl of the ultimate comfort food in her hands but another glass of bubbles… well…this was a rather different kettle of fish, that's what it was.

By the time he was scraping the last of his ice cream from the bowl, Noah had made a decision.

'I really need to get serious about finding a place to live that isn't just a room in a place that feels like it's part of my work environment,' he told Abby. 'I'd forgotten how important it is to be able to completely switch off sometimes.' He put his bowl on the table, swapping it for his glass of wine, and then he leaned back into this gloriously comfortable couch and let his breath out in a contented sigh. 'Somewhere like this would be perfect.'

'I do love this apartment,' Abby said. 'I had to move in with Lisa and Hugh for a while because there was so much work needed to renovate this place and make it wheelchair friendly, but it was such a relief to settle in here. It's taken twenty-six years but I feel like I'm finally living completely independently and I love it. The only thing missing is…maybe a cat. If I can find a ginger one, that is.'

'Why ginger? Oh…wait…' Noah shook his head. 'It's the family hair colour, isn't it?'

'Don't let anyone tell you you're not a smart man, Noah Baxter.' Abby handed him her bowl to put on the table and gave him both a smile and a nod when he offered her the other glass of wine he'd poured.

'And the newest family member—was Lisa's baby a boy or a girl?'

'A girl. She's been called Amy—after my gran.'

'And does she have red hair? I didn't notice the other night.'

'She's almost completely bald, so we can't tell yet.' Abby took a sip of her wine and then put her glass down. 'But I'm sure you don't want to be talking about babies. I... I'm sorry you got thrown into that situation. I know it can't have been easy for you.'

So she did know his story. Of course she did. He'd known that already, hadn't he? There was still no hint of pity in her eyes, though. Just understanding.

'It's fine,' he said quietly. 'It was a long time ago and life moves on. You find ways of coping. It wasn't that it upset me...it was more that I didn't want to intrude.'

It was a perfectly reasonable excuse for having excused himself so quickly that night but Noah was quite sure that Abby could sense everything he wasn't saying. She was still holding his gaze and it was a more intense version of the glance he'd caught as he'd slipped out the door when she'd been holding baby Amy. And an element in that look mixed with everything else this evening was providing—the welcoming feeling of home that this apartment had, sharing a meal and simply being able to relax in the company of someone who was trustworthy.

The result of that alchemy was something poignant that made Noah very aware of what would always be missing from his life because it was something that wasn't out of reach, it was more that he didn't have any desire to make the effort of reaching it. Maybe he wasn't even capable of stretching that far now.

He needed to break that eye contact. 'You see too much,' he murmured. 'I hope you're not going to tell me that telepathy is another one of your splinter skills.'

'I've never thought so.' Abby's voice was just as quiet as his. 'Until now.'

He still couldn't look away. Whatever it was that made it so easy to communicate with Abby worked both ways, didn't it? There was only one reason that she wanted a cat in her apartment and that was because she was lonely. She had the same empty space in her life as he did and, while Noah had accepted long ago that he would always have to live with that, Abby deserved better.

She was an absolutely stunning young woman and…and the way she was looking at him—the way it felt like she was touching something so deep that no one else could even see it—was pulling him in. Quite literally. Noah could feel himself leaning closer and closer to Abby.

And what happened then seemed as inevitable as taking his next breath.

He kissed her.

CHAPTER FIVE

DEAR LORD, BUT this man could kiss…

Abby had never been kissed like this before. Right now, it felt like no woman on earth had ever been kissed quite like this— with electrical currents of something fierce and totally irresistible that kept rippling through her body and, astonishingly, it actually felt like they were reaching parts that had been deprived of significant sensation her entire life.

She was so lost in this kiss, in the feel and taste and warmth and just how *alive* Noah's lips and mouth were, that Abby had no idea of how long it had gone on for. It was the tiny sound she made as she realised things were moving to the next level, when Noah's hand slipped down her arms and then brushed her breasts, that made it all come to a crashing halt. Noah jerked back as if he'd suddenly woken up.

For the longest moment, they both stared at each other. Abby was trying to catch her breath. Noah was pressing his fingers against his lips, as though he was trying to capture any remnants of that extraordinary kiss. Or perhaps he was stopping himself from kissing her again. Abby wanted to catch his fingers in her own. To bring them to touch her own lips. But she couldn't move and she couldn't look away.

'Sorry…' His voice was slightly muffled. 'I didn't mean…'

'You don't have to be sorry,' Abby said. 'And it doesn't have to mean anything… but…'

Another tiny pause without breaking that locked gaze and then Noah's eyebrow quirked—a silent request for her to finish what she was saying.

'But I liked it,' she said softly.

'Me, too…' But Noah was the one who broke the eye contact. 'Which feels weird because I was starting to think I'd never even want to kiss anyone else like that again.'

Abby could feel a stillness in the room.

As if they were both caught in a moment of time that could prove to be momentous. Life changing?

'That's a good thing, then,' she said carefully.

'Why?'

'Because I get the feeling that you're like me. That you might be lonely in a way that a friend or family can't be enough to fix and… and it would be sad to feel like that for the rest of our lives, wouldn't it?'

That got Noah's attention. His direct look was accompanied by a frown. 'I don't understand,' he said. 'You're gorgeous. Funny. Intelligent. A force to be reckoned with both on and off a basketball court. Surely you're only single because you're choosing to be?'

It was Abby's turn to break the eye contact. 'Yes…and no…,' she muttered. 'It's an old story and not one I particularly want to dredge up tonight. I'd rather talk about you. If anyone's got a legion of potential partners waiting in the wings, it's got to be you.'

Noah was silent for a moment. 'I can't go there,' he admitted. 'I'm not ready. And it's been so long now, maybe I never will be.'

'Because you think it might be a disaster

the first time?' Abby gulped the last of her wine. 'Tell me about it. It's not just the emotional risk—sex can be scary, right? I should know. I'm twenty-six and I've never... Oh... God...' She put her hand over her eyes. She hadn't drunk *that* much wine, surely? 'That's *way* too much information... I have no idea why I just told you that. Nobody else knows. Not even my sister...'

The silence was a lot longer this time. Abby could feel herself cringing.

'Sorry...' she muttered. 'I think I do know what you mean, though. We don't know each other that well yet but there's something there that...that's different. I feel like I can trust you and...and I really did like that kiss...'

When she risked a glance she found that Noah was watching her carefully. He held her gaze as soon as he caught it and when he reached out and touched her cheek so gently with his finger, it almost brought tears to her eyes.

'So did I,' he murmured.

His finger slipped from her cheek to trace a line to the back of her neck which he cupped with his hand. Slowly...agonisingly slowly, he bent his head to cover her lips again with his. But this time it was a more controlled kiss. It wasn't about to spiral into what Abby genuinely wanted—which was a lot more. More than a lot more, in fact. For the first time ever, despite every fear that might be trying to creep in from the back of her mind, she really did want it all.

He could feel exactly what Abby wanted through the touch of her lips and way her hands were shaping his shoulders and then his chest. He could even taste it and hear it in the way she was catching her breath and it was breaking his heart because…

Because she was amazing and she was trusting him with something so huge he didn't want to go there. Perhaps the reason she was still a virgin had something to do with her disability but not in the most obvious way. Noah had caught a nuance of something dark. That Abby was scared of sex because something had happened to scare her and that was…so sad. More than sad. The idea that someone could have treated her badly made a curl of anger stir in his gut.

When he broke this kiss, he cradled

her head in the dip below his collar bone. 'Don't be scared of sex, Abby,' he said. 'I don't know what your story is and you don't have to tell me but it *can* be wonderful. You shouldn't let it hold you back from a relationship.'

'But… I might be crap at it,' Abby whispered. 'Like I am with cooking. Or knitting.'

Noah smiled. 'It's not like that. You can't be bad at it. Not if you're with someone who cares.'

'It's a bit…different for me, though.' He could hear how difficult it was for Abby to get these words out as she paused to swallow hard. 'I mean…wouldn't it be… I don't know…*boring* to have sex with someone who can't move half her body?'

Oh, man… How could someone like Abby ever think that being with her could possibly be boring?

'Sex is about a lot more than what goes where and how you move,' he said softly. 'Most of it happens in here.' He touched his head. 'And, if you're lucky and you're with someone you're in love with, it happens in *here*.' This time he touched his chest over his heart.

'I'll have to get past the first time to find that out. And that first time will have to be with someone I could really trust.' Abby's head moved against his chest as she slid an upward glance at him. 'Like you.'

Noah had to close his eyes as he felt that sharp tug on his heartstrings. He lifted his hand to stroke her hair. 'I've never even really thought about being with anyone since Ellen died,' he told her. 'At first it was grief and then it was because I wasn't interested in anything other than my work. As I said, it's been a long time. So long, I couldn't be sure if I could go through with it. Now that you've mentioned it, it could well be a disaster waiting to happen.'

He could feel the tension increasing in Abby's muscles—as if she was gathering her courage?

'That makes two of us, then,' she said. 'And…don't you think it would be good to know? For…um…future reference? So that—if we ever wanted to—we wouldn't need to be nervous about whether or not it's even possible?'

'You mean like a trial run?'

'Exactly. No big deal...just a "friends helping each other out" kind of thing.'

It was a bad idea. A very bad idea. So why was his body trying to tell him something very different? For the first time in so long, things were falling into place, like a jigsaw puzzle. How attractive Abby was. How much he liked her company. How incredibly soft and delicious her mouth was. Oh, yeah...there were parts of his body feeling things that were intense enough to be bordering on pain.

'It's a bad idea.' At least his brain was being sensible. 'Not only because we have to work together. Your first time should be something special. With someone you're in love with and who's in love with you. So that it's making love and not just sex.'

'That's not going to happen.'

'You might be surprised.'

Abby shook her head. 'I'd be too nervous to let it happen.'

Noah could see those nerves in her eyes now. More than nerves. There was a hint of real fear there.

'What happened, Abby?' His voice was no more than a whisper. 'Did someone hurt you?'

Those glorious soft, brown eyes were shining as if tears were gathering. 'They tried to.' Her voice was as quiet as his. 'Someone I'd made the mistake of letting into the house after a first date. He was laughing that I couldn't run away. If Lisa hadn't come home a minute or two later, he would have…would have…'

Her voice was shaking. Noah put a gentle finger on her lips.

'I get it.'

He didn't need to know the details. He'd heard enough to know how scared she'd been and he could understand why she'd never gone there again. Anger towards the stranger who'd done this was strong enough to cause a wave of unpleasant heat but something else was even stronger. That Abby was trusting *him* to exorcise those ghosts of the past? He had to swallow past a lump in his throat. He already thought enough of Abby to believe she deserved the best things that life had to offer but she was going to miss out on so much if she couldn't learn that being close to someone didn't need to be terrifying. It was a gift that she was asking him to provide.

And…as unlikely as it had seemed before

he'd met Abby, his body was continuing to wake up. Telling him that he, too, was missing something in his life that was important. He didn't have to think about falling in love with someone or getting married again but…well…sex was just a part of a normal life, wasn't it? And he really wanted to kiss Abby again. To touch her. To make her feel special. To…hopefully…take them both over the edge. This was totally different from any sexual experience he would have ever had before.

New ground.

But he shook his head. 'We can't. I don't carry anything these days. Protection, that is.'

'There are condoms on the top shelf of my bathroom cupboard,' Abby told him. She even found a hint of smile. An embarrassed but mischievous kind of smile. 'I know… but Lisa looks in there sometimes. I didn't want her thinking I didn't have any kind of sex life, you know?'

Okay…that smile did it. Or maybe it was the humour behind a statement that covered an issue that was huge but that she was dealing with all by herself. The courage of this woman blew him away and Noah was responding to that on both an emotional and physical level as he kissed her yet again. He pushed himself up off the sofa a minute or two later.

'I'll be right back,' he murmured.

'So…how did it go?'

'Sorry…what?' Abby looked up from the bundle of sleeping baby in her arms to meet her sister's gaze. Surely Lisa wasn't reading her mind? How embarrassing would it be if she'd guessed what Abby was thinking about right then—that last night had been so much better than the first time she and Noah had been together.

Not that that first time on the couch had not been good. He'd been so reassuring about how attractive she was and so gentle, letting Abby set the pace and encouraging her to show him how to help position her legs and make it all possible but, if she was really honest, there had been elements of both awkwardness and…yeah…remnants of fear and the kind of momentary flashbacks that had always been enough to make sure she never went that far again.

But not last night. Oh, no… They'd used her bed last night and there'd been laughter involved. Jokes about just needing a bit more practice to make sure that Abby was confident with her new splinter skill. And the balance between caution and passion had changed. They were more comfortable with each other's bodies. More ready to take risks and…well…they'd paid off.

If Abby had ever wondered—and, of course, she had—whether the amount of sensation she had in her lower body could allow a partner to generate that ultimate release of sexual tension, then she'd certainly found out last night.

Did it show in her face or something?

Lisa was shaking her head at Abby's apprehensive expression. 'For heaven's sake… I'm the one who's sleep-deprived and has mush for brains. I mean that surgery that is the talk of St John's at the moment. The toe to thumb thing. How did it go yesterday?'

'Oh…' Abby let out a relieved breath. She would no doubt tell her sister about this new development in her personal life very soon but she wasn't ready to just yet. It was too new. Too…precious?

No, that wasn't quite the right word. It wasn't as if she and Noah were in a relationship or anything. This was purely a friendship, albeit with a bit of a crush on her side, and the sex had been only supposed to be a one-off—an experiment to see if either of them was ready or even capable of enjoying it. And then it had been another one-off last night—just to see if improvements in technique could be made.

'The surgery was amazing. *Noah* was amazing.' Abby couldn't keep the note of pride from her voice. 'I only got to watch part of it but it was incredible. There was a huge team in Theatre—I've never seen so many people involved in one operation but they all worked together seamlessly. And some of what they did was just mind-blowing—joining those tiny nerves and blood vessels together. So delicate and painstaking. Like a form of art, really…'

'Hmm…' Lisa coming towards where Abby had positioned her wheelchair. 'Noah Baxter has certainly impressed you, hasn't he?'

Abby's shrug was muted because she had her arms full of baby Amy. 'He's very good at what he does,' she said. 'Everybody knows that.'

Not everybody knew about everything he was so good at, though. She was the first woman Noah had made love to since he'd lost his wife. That made it special, didn't it?

Made Abby special?

No…she couldn't start thinking like that, although it was hard not to. Especially after last night, when her trust in Noah had been taken to a whole new level. When they could make each other laugh, even in the midst of something that felt so significant.

So life-changing.

The baby stirred in Abby's arms and whimpered. Both women were instantly focused on the infant and Abby knew that Lisa's interest in Noah Baxter, or even Steve's much talked about surgery had faded. As she was rocked, Amy settled back to sleep, her tiny mouth pouting and then relaxing again and even curling up at the corners.

'Look at that…she's smiling.'

'It's too early.' Lisa shook her head. 'They don't smile until they're about six weeks old. Must be wind.'

But baby Amy seemed to want to prove

her mother wrong by repeating her facial twist and, this time, Lisa reached for her phone. 'Hugh's not going to believe this,' she said. 'Try rocking her again and I'll take a video.'

But Abby had to pause to drop a soft kiss onto her niece's head. 'She's so adorable,' she told Lisa. 'I think I want one.'

'Be careful what you wish for,' Lisa warned. 'I've never been so tired in all my life. She'd being an angel right now but it's a different story at three a.m., believe me.'

Rocking didn't produce anything like a smile this time. Instead, Amy woke up and let her mother know in no uncertain terms that she needed attention. Her cries got rapidly louder as Lisa took her from Abby's arms and settled into another chair to feed her.

'How can something that adorable make a noise like that?'

'It's worse at three a.m.' But Lisa was smiling as she nestled Amy into the crook of her arm and helped her latch on to her breast.

'I take it back,' Abby decided. 'Or at least I'll postpone it a lot longer. I don't want one yet.'

'You can enjoy this one,' Lisa told her. 'So much better when you can go home when you've had enough. In the meantime, could you get the nappy-changing supplies? She's going to need some clean pants after this.'

Abby moved towards the bag of nappies and wipes that were being kept downstairs to save a trip up to the nursery on the first floor of this huge, old house. She was quite happy to postpone parenthood. She needed to follow her sister's example and find the perfect man to father a baby, anyway. At least she was confident that that could happen now. She had, after all, found the perfect first lover in a physical sense, hadn't she? It was such a shame that Noah was nowhere near ready to consider a "real" relationship but that was simply the way things were and Abby totally respected that. She was envious of a love that was so strong it could continue after death, in fact, and never be replaced. Just the kind of love she would have to hope that she, too, could find one day.

'Fantastic.' Noah could feel his smile stretching enough to light up his face as he observed the small but controlled range of movement in the thumb that had only ever been a big toe before. 'Exactly what I would be hoping for at this stage of your intensive therapy, Steve, and it's only been two weeks of stepping up the pace.'

'A bit over ten weeks since my surgery.' Steve nodded. 'I'm even walking without much of a limp now.'

'Show me?'

Steve was sitting at a table in a treatment room of the hand clinic, with Abby beside him. His wife Pauline was in a corner of the room, the baby on her lap and a toddler playing with some toys at her feet. Noah had seen them through the window in the door as he'd passed so he'd come in, just to offer encouragement to his patient. And, okay, maybe because it was an excuse to spend a little bit of time with Abby at work. He caught her gaze as Steve stood up to walk the length of the room and back, automatically cradling his injured hand with his other arm to protect it as he moved.

Noah could see Abby's satisfaction in her patient's progress in her eyes. He could also see the pleasure that his surprise visit was creating and, on a level beneath that, how strong their friendship had become.

He'd never met anyone with whom so much communication could happen with a glance that lasted only a heartbeat or two, and it still surprised him even though he'd had more than a couple of months to get used to it. Kind of like the way that sex with Abby still surprised him every single time— because there was always something a little different about it? A new note of discovery or depth or maybe just…delight. Something new, anyway.

Something different enough to have made flashbacks almost a thing of the past and to make it feel like Noah was genuinely moving forward with his life in some way. And, whatever it was, neither of them had quite had enough even though the "one-off" joke had worn off so long ago that neither of them bothered bringing it up now. It wasn't as if they saw each other that often. Once a week at the most—usually after a training session for wheelchair basketball at the gym—and nobody would guess there was anything more than friendship between them if they saw them together at work.

Although Noah found himself turning his head, aware of Pauline's steady gaze, and there was a look on her face that made him wonder if she might have guessed there was more than something strictly professional in his relationship with Abby. Steve certainly wasn't aware of anything other than showing the two main medical professionals still involved with his case how well he was now walking. He had supportive strapping and a shoe insert on the foot where the toe had been removed but his work with a physiotherapist was adjusting his gait enough to make any change almost indiscernible.

'That's brilliant,' Noah told him. 'I can see how much effort you're putting into your rehabilitation.'

'It's my job,' Steve said. 'Until I can get back to my real job, that is. And I need to do that as soon as I can. The benefits aren't enough, you know?'

'We're managing.' Pauline spoke up. 'I'm not going to say it's easy but we'll get there.'

Steve nodded. 'It's helping being at home again. I'm not about to lose my motivation when I've got the kids in front of me all the time.'

'How's the sensory rehab going?'

Steve and Abby shared a glance. 'Not so great,' he said. 'I can't tell the difference between sandpaper and cotton wool if I've got my eyes closed.'

'We're putting a bag together,' Abby added. She waved her hand at a tray of small objects on one side of the table that included a marble, coin, strip of the hooked side of Velcro and some soft fabric. 'For homework. It can be a game with one of your older children, Steve—where they let you feel something with your eyes open and then again with your eyes closed when you try and guess what it is.' She smiled at the toddler sitting by Pauline's feet. 'You could play that game with Daddy, Lucy, couldn't you?'

Pauline ruffled her daughter's curls. 'She could. And her big brother, Mack, would just love it, too.'

Her smile at Abby made Noah realise that bonds were being formed that were wider than simply between a patient and his therapist. There was gratitude there as well. Because the whole family was being included in the therapy for a beloved husband and father? He'd always known that Abby was good at her job but this was a reminder of just how special she was—in so many ways.

Steve's smile was wry. 'Mack *will* love that. Something he can beat me in until we can play footie again.'

'You can also try and get them out of the bag yourself,' Abby told him. 'It'll be good exercise for your whole hand. Let's give it a try now, shall we?'

Pauline looked up to catch Noah's gaze as Abby gathered the objects to put them into the bag and she was still smiling. In fact, there was a hint of a gleam in her eyes that suggested that if he'd been right in his suspicion that she thought there was possibly something going on between himself and Abby, Pauline approved of it.

He needed to dispel any notion that had the potential to turn into an unwelcome rumour. This clearly needed a more definitively professional note.

'I'll leave you to it,' Noah told them, a little more abruptly than he'd intended, as he turned to leave. 'But I'm glad I saw you today, Steve. I'll look forward to the next progress report when you come into Outpatients. Keep up the great work.'

* * *

'What's up, Abby?' Lisa had a concerned frown on her face. 'You don't look so great.'

'I dunno. Maybe I overdid it at training last night. Or maybe I've just gone off mushy peas. How did I ever like something that looks like it's been pre-chewed?'

'Is everything else okay? Like with…you know who?' Lisa lowered her voice as she looked over her shoulder to where Hugh was peering into the fridge in the hope of finding a beer to go with his takeout curry.

Abby frowned. She had confessed a while back to her "friendship with benefits", but had made her sister swear that she wouldn't breathe a word, even to her husband. It was for that reason she'd been relieved that Hugh hadn't invited Noah again to share their weekly family takeout night. It had been a one-off. Like the sex had been supposed to be?

Abby sighed as she stared her pot of mushy peas. Even if Hugh was also sworn to secrecy it might only take a meaningful glance at the wrong time to start some gossip at the hospital and that was the last thing Abby wanted. Because she knew it would be the last thing that Noah would want. Look at the way he'd rushed out of the room when Pauline had been watching them a little too closely that time he'd come in to see how Steve's therapy was going.

Or maybe it was because she still wasn't ready to stop their intimate time together. At some point in the last few weeks, even though she had been quite determined to keep that crush under control, the dreams had started to creep back and the idea that she might have actually started to fall in love with Noah Baxter on the day she'd met him was also refusing to be entirely shut down. It was a worry and that was probably adding to whatever it was that was upsetting Abby's normal approach to life.

'We're completely out of anything to drink. Beer *or* wine.' Hugh sounded disappointed. 'And it's the first night that Amy's gone to sleep early enough for us to have dinner together properly.'

'There's an off-licence five minutes away,' Lisa told him. 'Go and get something. We can keep the food warm. It's Friday night and Abby looks like she could do with a glass of wine.'

But Abby shook her head. 'Not for me, thanks.'

'Not even some bubbles?' Hugh was grinning as he reached out to touch Abby's forehead. 'You're not coming down with something, are you?'

'Go,' Lisa ordered. 'The sooner you're back, the sooner we can eat.'

'Don't bother keeping the peas warm,' Abby said as Lisa collected the containers to put in the oven. 'I don't think I'm even hungry any more. Maybe I'll go home and let you and Hugh have a romantic evening together. You never know, you might get enough time for more than dinner.'

'Are you kidding?' Lisa flopped back into her chair and closed her eyes. 'I'm too tired to even *think* about sex these days. I have no idea how people get round to having a second child.'

Abby smiled but it was her turn to frown. Was she doing enough to help her sister in this happy but stressful time with a new baby? Because she was focused on Lisa's face she saw the moment her eyes suddenly opened again to glance at the pot of mushy peas and then catch Abby's gaze. She also saw the expression of something like alarm.

'You're not pregnant, are you? That could be why you've suddenly gone off something.'

'Of course not. Don't be daft.'

'Well…it's not as if it's not possible. You're the one who's getting some action in that "good friendship" of yours.' Lisa used her fingers to create quotation marks.

Abby glared at her. She didn't like her sex life being referred to as nothing more than a bit of "action", even if that was exactly what it was supposed to be. 'I'm not stupid, Lise. We've always used condoms.'

'Not that supply from your bathroom cupboard, I hope.'

Abby's glare deepened. What on earth was Lisa referring to now? And they'd only used hers the first time, anyway.

Lisa shrugged. 'Hey, it's not my fault they fell off the shelf when I needed some dental floss. And I'm a nurse, remember. I'm trained to notice expiry dates. Those condoms of yours expired way before you even moved into that apartment.'

They *had* been around for a long time. Because they'd never been used. But Abby shook her head. 'It wouldn't make any difference. We all know some things last way beyond expiry dates.'

'And we all know some things can fail occasionally.' Lisa's voice was quiet now. 'I've got some pregnancy test kits somewhere in *my* bathroom cupboard. Maybe you should take one home with you. Just in case. And you don't need to worry, I'm not about to say anything to Hugh.'

She didn't need to worry?

She'd thought that rumours of how far their friendship had gone would be the last thing Noah would want?

How wrong was it possible for someone to be?

Back home in her own apartment later that evening, in the privacy of her own bathroom, Abby was staring at what she held in her hands. At the tiny plastic window that was showing two distinct lines. At the helpful print beside the window that had an image of a single line beside the words "Not Pregnant" and one of the double lines with that single word "Pregnant" beside it.

A word that was sounding repeatedly in

Abby's head right now. Like a bell. One with a tone that was deep enough to sound menacing. She had no idea how long she sat there listening to it before making the effort to move, taking the evidence of what she'd just discovered so that she could hide it in the kitchen rubbish bin. She was shaking her head as she went.

She'd known that losing her virginity might change her life.

A sound like wry laughter escaped her lips as she reached the kitchen.

She hadn't been wrong, had she? Neither had Lisa. Her sister had been more right than she'd realised when she'd told her she needed to be careful about what she wished for when Abby had said she thought she wanted a baby, although admitting that was not going to give either of them any kind of satisfaction.

And as for telling Noah…

Well… Abby couldn't even begin to think about that. At least she had a whole weekend to start trying to get her head around this before she had to go back to work. Probably even longer before she was breathing the same air as Noah, but it wouldn't be long enough. She was never going to be ready to deliver news that she knew would be devastating for him. He had trusted that, even though they had carried on for longer than intended, what they had was no more than a temporary arrangement. Friends helping each other out as a favour so that they would both know it was possible to move into a new stage of their lives when the time was right.

That time was not now.

Not for Abby and most definitely not for Noah.

CHAPTER SIX

IT SEEMED THAT the more you looked for excuses, the easier it became to find them, but the point at which it became obvious that something was being avoided was inevitably going to arrive. And there was only so long you could put off doing something that you knew had to be done, no matter how hard you knew it was going to be.

It was no big deal to avoid seeing Noah that next week. All Abby needed to do was to say she was too busy to go to basketball training, which was partly true because she'd been tasked with starting an update on all the information pamphlets that the hand clinic made available for their patients. Currently, she was working on an activity list for people recovering from injury or surgery on their hands so that they would know what was permissible when instructed to keep to light or moderate activities, as well as the information given to people facing surgery for carpal tunnel syndrome.

Abby had convinced herself that there was no great urgency in telling Noah. She'd only done a home test and even Lisa had said that she should not only repeat it but have a more definitive blood test done.

She also needed more information before she would be able to answer the questions that Noah would undoubtedly have—like how far along in her pregnancy she was. Abby had no idea, but if she was at a really early stage, she might have to consider whether or not she needed to tell him at all, given his tragic history and how this could affect him. It was obviously going to affect their friendship and, while it was new, it was something that Abby didn't want to lose.

The possibility that she might decide she simply wasn't ready for parenthood because of her age or career or disability or the fact that she was lacking a life partner might be something she didn't want to consider yet but it would have to be faced soon. Time was not her friend right now.

She could legitimately claim that she was too busy treating a patient to stop and talk to Noah on an occasion when he happened to visit the clinic in the days before the appointment she had booked. She knew that he'd been told that she was at a doctor's appointment the following week when she'd missed the team meeting about new patients but she also knew that none of her colleagues had any idea that her appointment was with an obstetrician rather than any of the more usual members of the medical team that had looked after her for most of her life.

It was, therefore, more than a little disconcerting to find Noah, with a worried frown on his face, at the door of her office later that same afternoon. As she stared at him, unable to find a smile, he came inside and closed the door behind him.

'I just came to check that you're okay,' he said. 'You missed the team meeting.'

'I'm fine,' Abby told him. Which was true. Pregnancy wasn't an illness, after all, and she had an echo in the back of her mind reminding her that being less than truthful was far more convincing if at least a part of it was accurate.

'But you had a doctor's appointment today.'

'Just a check-up.' Abby turned to rearrange the papers on her desk. The element of truth thing might be forgivable when you were trying to pass off a store-bought meal as home cooking but she was running out of excuses now. She had all the information she needed.

And Noah needed to know the real truth. Even if she was still having trouble processing everything she had learned today herself. In a way, it was a relief that she was already past the point where an option to make this all disappear would have been relatively straightforward but that was shocking in itself because she was that much closer to her life changing for ever. To becoming a mother...

'I have something for you,' Noah said.

Abby tried to smile as she took the manila folder from his hand. She had something for him as well but, for the life of her, she couldn't find the words she needed to drop the bombshell that his life was also about to change for ever. She couldn't find the courage to deliver those words either. Maybe that was because work was definitely not the right place? With an inward sigh of relief, she focused on the distraction immediately at hand.

'Oh…these are the photos we talked about a couple of weeks ago.' When everything had been as it should be in her world. Better than that, in fact. She'd had it all. Her wonderful job and apartment. A demanding sport to keep her fit. A new niece to treasure and a new friendship that was so special it was also something to be treasured.

'We had a carpal tunnel day surgery session this morning. I had someone from Medical Illustrations come up and take the photos of the endoscopic procedure, which is what the majority of patients will have here now. I'd only consider open surgery if there's a tumour or some other growth to deal with. Or scar tissue from a previous injury or surgery perhaps.'

Abby nodded. She was sifting through papers on her desk to find the relevant pamphlet she'd been tweaking.

'Have you got a minute to check some of the text I've changed? Oh…and I wondered about using a different anatomical diagram to identify the ligament that gets cut.'

'That diagram is fine,' Noah said, as he pulled a chair closer and sat down beside Abby. 'But I'd label it the transverse carpal ligament rather than the flexor retinaculum. This information is intended for laypeople, yes?'

'Mmm…' The word "information" was reminding Abby of what she had to share and she bit her bottom lip as she watched Noah scanning the rest of the text in the updated pamphlet. This wasn't an appropriate time. Not that there was ever going to be a *good* time but Noah, especially, was someone who preferred to keep his personal and professional lives completely separate. She couldn't say anything. Not here. Not now.

'That's a good description of endoscopic surgery, saying that there's a tiny camera through one cut and the other one is used to guide the instrument that cuts the ligament. One of today's photos will be ideal to go with that paragraph. I'd add in a bit about it only needing local anaesthetic and it being a day procedure.'

'What about risks?'

'I can give you some percentage data. Basically, there's more risk of nerve damage with an endoscopic procedure rather than open surgery but it's almost always temporary and recovery time is less. On average, people are back at work about nine days sooner. And there's much less risk of scar tenderness.'

'I won't go into too much detail. That's something patients can discuss with their surgeons. It'll vary so much between cases anyway—like how much time they're going to need off work. I've said it can be anything from one to eight weeks depending on whether it's a dominant hand and how much repetitive manual work is required.'

Abby was about to point out one of the introductory paragraphs of the pamphlet where there was information about the non-surgical treatment of carpal tunnel syndrome, such as steroid injections, splints and ultrasound, that would be tried for some time before surgery was considered, when she became aware that she was being watched. Closely.

'Are you sure you're okay, Abby? You do look a bit pale.'

'Do I?'

'Mmm. And, I may be wrong, but it feels

as if you've been avoiding me lately. Have I said something to upset you?'

'No…not at all…'

'Then what is it? You can tell me, you know. We're friends, aren't we?'

Oh, boy…being under the intense gaze of those dark, dark eyes was doing something weird to Abby's stomach. As if the butterflies that came with sexual attraction were being buffeted by powerful currents generated by a churning sensation that could well become nausea. It was unbearable, in fact, and the words that Abby had been finding impossible to form suddenly came rushing from her throat into her mouth and beyond with such force that it was astonishing they escaped as no more than a whisper.

'I'm pregnant…'

They were so close. She could see the moment that Noah's brain processed her words. She could see the shaft of shock and then pain that followed almost instantly. Was he remembering the last time someone had told him he was going to become a father? The joy that had become such an unbearable tragedy a few months later?

She was doing this to him. She was causing this pain and Abby hated herself for it. More than that, she wanted nothing more than to wrap her arms around Noah so that she could do her best to absorb that pain for him. To protect him. To promise that she would do anything to try and help.

And it was in that moment that Abby realised just how much she loved Noah. This wasn't the kind of love that came from friendship—even one that happened to include some pretty amazing sex. It certainly didn't come from a transitory crush. This was the kind of love that came from a place that included the permanence of family. From caring so much about someone that you would choose to spend the rest of your life with them.

This was about being *in* love.

And it was heartbreaking because she could see so clearly what she had known all along—that there was no way Noah was ever going to feel the same way about her. He was looking so shocked right now.

Appalled, even…

'But…we were careful…'

Abby closed her eyes. 'It might have been that first time. My secret stash had been in the cupboard for a long time. Years. I'm so sorry... It didn't occur to me that they might have gone so far past their expiry date—'

'The *first* time?' Noah had clearly only heard her first sentence. 'But...but that's more than two months ago.'

'I had a scan this afternoon,' Abby admitted. 'It looks like I'm into my second trimester so it would fit. I'm a bit over thirteen weeks.'

Noah was looking at her now as if she'd stepped into this room from another planet.

'I had some spotting,' she told him. 'My period's usually light and my cycle's not that regular anyway. It didn't even occur to me until...'

Until Lisa had wondered why she'd thought the mushy peas looked so horrible...

But she couldn't say that. Because it reminded her of the night that Noah had been there to share a takeaway dinner on his first day working at St John's and he'd joked that she was into healthy food. The night that connection with their passion for their work and their friendship had been born. A friendship that had rapidly led to a whole lot more and was now tumbling down around them into such a total disaster that Abby knew she was about to burst into tears.

Noah looked just as upset. He was as white as a sheet and the pamphlet he'd been holding was slipping from his hand to hit the floor and slide towards Abby's wheelchair.

It was the knock on her door that broke that awful moment as they stared at each other with neither of them knowing what to say next. Abby ducked, to hide her face from whoever was about to come into her office, holding onto her wheel so that she could lean down far enough to pick up that pamphlet.

'Ah... I'm so glad you're still here, Noah.' It was Alex, the orthopaedic registrar. 'I couldn't borrow your expertise for a second opinion, could I? I've got a chap in my clinic outpatients and he's got a post-surgical complication. A wound breakdown that I don't like the look of at all.'

As Abby straightened, she could see the effort that it took for Noah to replace something intensely personal with the mantle of professionalism. She could see the remnants of that private pain being swept from his face and replaced by a mask that would reveal nothing before he turned towards the door.

'Of course, Alex.' Only Abby would notice the extra effort that went into pushing himself to his feet—as if even that ordinary action was physically painful. 'Your timing is perfect, in fact. Abby and I have finished our discussion for the moment, haven't we?'

He didn't wait for a response or even look at her as he joined Alex at the door and then disappeared down the corridor. He was right, of course. There would be plenty of time to discuss other things in the weeks and months to come.

Clearly, Noah had already heard a lot more than he wanted to for now. Abby didn't realise she had been holding her breath until it came out in a long sigh. At least the first step had been taken and she had told him. She knew it would have brought back terrible memories for him and that he was hurting but this would be the worst of it, surely? When he'd had time to get over the shock, they could talk again. In the meantime, Abby needed someone else to talk to.

Her big sister. The closest thing to a mother she'd ever had, in fact. Lisa had been six years old when Abby was born and right from the start she'd been her guardian. After her accident, Lisa had pretty much centred her life around her younger sister. It was time to tell her everything because she really needed to be with someone who would be on her side. Who loved her unconditionally, as much as she loved them.

Abby gathered up the photographs Noah had brought and the outlines for the updated pamphlet and stuffed them into her laptop bag. Not that she was likely to do any work this evening but looking like she intended to work at home gave her an excuse to leave her office a little early. And this way she wouldn't have to face Noah again just yet. The least she could do for him right now was to give him some time and space to get his head around what must feel like his worst nightmare.

If only this was simply a bad dream and he was going to wake up soon.

As a form of escape, Noah had focused so completely on Alex's patient that it was quite some time before anything personal had a chance to cross those barriers and fill his head. An ultrasound and other tests on the young man who'd had orthopaedic surgery on his arm and hand following a motor-bike accident showed that he had developed blood clots that were compromising blood supply enough to cause the wound break-down. Not only that, the wounds were now infected and urgent treatment was needed if the patient wasn't going to lose significant hand function. Noah even stayed to work with the orthopaedic team in Theatre to re-move the clots, debride the wounds and re-pair them.

So it was already late by the time he left the hospital and went to his room in the staff quarters where there was no escaping the fact that what Abby had told him was not going to evaporate like any normal night-mare. This was a small, stark room in com-parison to Abby's spacious apartment but Noah hadn't yet found the time or inclina-tion to go searching for more permanent ac-commodation.

Maybe, deep down, he'd known he might not be staying here that long. How could he stay now that he was faced with the one thing he'd been determined never to go through again? This wasn't new ground any more. This was history repeating itself in the worst possible way. The prospect of fatherhood, with all the responsibility and implications for the future that that entailed, along with the fear that came with knowing exactly how catastrophic it could be when things went wrong.

But then again…how could he *not* stay here? It was his baby that Abby was carrying. His child. As much as a huge part of him wanted to flee, he could never, ever contemplate running away from that reality.

But even the thought of becoming a father again was tearing his heart into pieces. He could remember that fierce joy and rush of love that had managed to puncture a numbing grief when he'd been allowed to hold his tiny infant in his arms for just a brief moment before she had been whisked away to the neonatal intensive care unit. And he could remember the agony of being allowed to hold her again as she'd taken her final breaths, when all those wires and tubes had been removed because it had been so obvious that nothing more could be done to keep her alive.

Oh… *God*…

He couldn't stay shut in here with thoughts

that were threatening to overwhelm him more than they had in years now. A full-on session of wheelchair basketball training would have been ideal to quash such unbearable memories and burn off emotions Noah didn't want to have to deal with but that wasn't an option tonight. It might never be an option again, in fact, because it felt like his friendship with Abby and everything that had come with that had just exploded in a fiery crash he hadn't seen coming.

What he could do was what he'd done in the past to relieve stress and that was to run. Hard and fast, for as long as he could before exhaustion forced him to stop. Within minutes, Noah had changed and he was pounding the pavement that circled a local park—trying, but failing, to outrun the thoughts circling in his head.

This pain was never going to go away, was it? The reminders were far less frequent, of course, and the pain was less raw but it was something he'd never forget. Something he'd never, ever want to experience again, and the only guarantee that that could never happen had just been taken away from him. Shards of memory were repeatedly piercing whatever mantle of protection that hard exercise like this could normally provide.

He could remember everything in a kind of reverse order. The funeral where Ellen had been buried with her tiny baby in her arms. Those terrible hours in the neonatal intensive care unit. The trauma of his wife's death and the shocking way their child had been delivered. The excitement in Ellen's eyes as she'd told him she was pregnant. But there'd been a question there as well, because it hadn't exactly been a planned pregnancy. She had wondered if he was going to be just as happy about it as she was. Whether it was the right time.

There'd been more than a question in Abby's eyes today. Like the way she'd understood what it had been like for him to be in Lisa's room so soon after the birth of her baby, it seemed that she knew exactly how hard it was going to be for him to be told he was going to be a father again. She had been feeling his pain and it was hurting her as well because...because she cared about him? *Loved* him, even?

He cared about Abby too. Not in the same way as he'd cared about Ellen, of course—he could never love anyone like that again—but he had absolute admiration for Abby and she was the closest friend he'd ever had. Because he'd never had a friendship that included sex before? Well…that had clearly been a mistake, hadn't it?

Except that it still didn't feel like a mistake. It had been so different. So… No… Noah couldn't think of a word that could encompass how it had made him feel to be with Abby. To feel that connection that was unlike anything he'd found before. To feel the trust that had blossomed into an eagerness to learn everything he could teach her about enjoying her body. To give as much as she was receiving and to do it with humour and a tenderness that had touched him in far more than a purely physical way.

He hadn't even asked her how she was feeling about the news today. Or if she was okay physically. Or what the implications of pregnancy and birth might be for a paraplegic woman. As he kept running, Noah tried to remember whether Ellen had had anything that had been a physical problem in her pregnancy but that period of his life was oddly blurry now. Instead of seeing Ellen in his head, he kept seeing Abby. Images that were brightly coloured instead of faded pastels. A living person rather than a ghost?

And he'd just walked out on her. As if he was the only one whose life was going to be changed for ever. How selfish was that? It was Abby who was going to be dealing with a lot more than he would have to and she was going to face more challenges than most pregnant women or new mothers.

Noah not only had a responsibility to a baby he wasn't about to turn his back on, right now he had even more of a responsibility to the mother of his child and, by the time he'd completed his third circuit of the park, Noah knew what he had to do. What the right thing to do was. He might have learned to shut himself away from grief but he wasn't about to try and bury guilt as well. Nothing could change what had given him so much grief but at least he had the power to change what would create guilt. He went back to his room to shower and change and then he walked the short distance to Abby's apartment and rang her bell.

He rang it again but there was still no answer.

He could see there were no lights on in her ground-floor apartment either.

She wasn't home. As Noah stood there, wondering where Abby might be and how long it might be before she came home, he could hear his stomach growling and remembered that he hadn't bothered eating this evening. It would be sensible to go and find some food but he wasn't going anywhere because it was far more important to talk to Abby. To tell her that he was going to be involved in their baby's life as much as she wanted him to be. That he would do everything he could to support her as well.

Noah sat down on the step beside the wheelchair ramp. He was going to wait until Abby came home because he didn't want her to spend the night thinking he had simply walked out on her and the future she now faced.

His commitment had been made and he wasn't about to walk away from anything, no matter how hard it might be.

He still looked shell shocked.

But there was something about the tilt of his head and the way he got to his feet so deliberately as Abby approached that told her he was in control again and that he was going to face whatever lay ahead with dignity, kindness and probably the kind of humour she had learned was something they both used as a defence against the more difficult challenges life could throw at you. She felt so proud of him at this moment it made her want to cry. How could you not fall in love with a man that was this courageous? This honourable?

This life challenge was a doozy but Noah was here. He might have been here for some time while she'd been with Lisa, just waiting for her to come home, and that made her heart squeeze painfully because it felt like he really cared—about her and not just the baby or whatever arrangements needed to be made for the future.

'You'd better come inside,' Abby told Noah. 'I'm so sorry. I had no idea you would be here. I went to visit Lisa and Hugh.' She led the way up the ramp. 'I thought you'd need time to…to think about things.'

'I did,' Noah agreed. 'And I still do. I'm sure you do as well. But we're in this together, Abby, and I wanted to make sure you knew that.'

There was no wine tonight. No firelight. Even the sexual attraction that had brought them to this situation seemed to have been snuffed out like a candle in an unexpected gust of wind. They avoided the squashy couches in the living area and sat on either side of Abby's kitchen table.

'How are you?' Noah asked. 'I'm sorry I didn't ask earlier. That should have been the first thing I checked on. How you're doing. How the…baby's doing.'

'I'm fine. Everything looks normal. They'll do another scan in three or four weeks. You can come with me if…if you want to.'

She could see the muscles in Noah's throat move as if it was difficult for him to swallow. 'Of course. If I can…' He cleared his throat. 'Are there any problems you might be facing because of your…your…?'

'Disability?' Abby's smile was wry. 'It's not a dirty word, Noah.'

He still looked so pale, she thought. The lines around his eyes were so much deeper. She wanted to touch him and offer comfort but she knew how unlikely that was to be welcome so she pushed her hands down to hide between her hips and the low sides of her chair as she curled them into fists.

'There are some things that may be a problem,' she admitted. 'As the baby grows it'll put pressure on my bladder, which may change the way I can manage. I might get bladder spasms and a urinary tract infection could trigger premature labour.'

Noah was nodding. He was finding this easier, wasn't he? A medical scenario to think about instead of an emotional one.

'I could get increased pressure on venous return from my legs so it puts me at increased risk of a deep vein thrombosis. I might have to wear some of those very sexy compression stockings.'

Her attempt at any kind of humour was falling flat. A bit like first time when he'd been so worried about whether she'd been hurt in that minor car accident and she'd told him she'd never walk again. Her heart was squeezing again as she remembered seeing him for the first time. Already starting to fall in love with him...

'Apart from that, it might interfere with my centre of balance in later stages and I'll need to adapt, but I've got plenty of time to get used to that.'

'You'll need help,' Noah said. 'Maybe I can help by organising a housekeeper? Or… someone to help *you*…?'

'I'm still perfectly independent,' Abby told him. 'And that's the way I intend to stay.'

This felt like Noah was seeing her disability as a barrier—maybe for the first time? He hadn't even seen it to start with. He hadn't let it interfere with their professional relationship in any way. Or their friendship. Okay, he'd needed to get used to a different kind of sex life perhaps, but that hadn't seemed to lessen the satisfaction he'd got from their time together and that reassurance had been just one of the gifts he'd given her.

Oh…if only he'd reach out and touch her now. Or better yet wrap her in his arms and take her to bed. Not for sex necessarily, but just to lie there and have this discussion like two people who cared deeply for each other and wanted a future together.

She could hear the sharp tone that came into her voice. The kind of prickly, defensive response that had always made men back off. 'If I do find I need help I can organise it myself, thanks. I also have a supportive family with Lisa and Hugh. I won't be the first disabled woman to have a baby, you know.'

Abby could feel Noah becoming cautious. Not knowing what to say.

'I wasn't suggesting you couldn't cope, Abby. I…just want to help…'

'Because I'm *disabled*.'

'No…' Was he going to become angry if she kept pushing this? 'Because I'm involved. Because I *care*…'

Not enough… Abby tried to push the silent cry away. Was she trying to find a way to push Noah away as well? To make herself believe that it didn't matter that he wasn't in love with her and never would be? To protect her heart as much as possible?

'I'm tired,' she said. 'I think it would be better if you left. I'll see you at work, obviously, but we both need time to get used to this. We can talk about other things some other time. I'll keep you posted on any medical appointments and, if you want to be there, that's fine.'

Noah got slowly to his feet. 'I'll be there.'

'I won't be going to basketball training sessions any longer. Not until after the birth anyway.' Abby followed Noah to her front door. 'There's no reason for you to stop going, though.'

'I won't be going either.'

Noah paused for a heartbeat on the step. When he turned, the expression in those dark eyes made Abby realise that he'd put up barriers. The kind she'd seen him use in his professional relationships at work where he gave nothing away, but it was something new when they were alone together. And it hurt. Knowing that he needed to protect himself from her broke Abby's heart that little bit more.

But surely the bond of their friendship was still there?

When Noah paused again at street level, looked back and raised his hand in farewell, the way the corner of his mouth lifted in a half-smile gave Abby a beat of hope that she was right. That at least a part of that friendship might be intact. That the reason he wasn't going to continue with a new sport that he really enjoyed was because she wasn't going to be there with him.

They also had a new bond that would be there for the rest of their lives.

It wasn't the kind of bond either of them would have chosen and it felt fragile and difficult. But it was there.

And perhaps it was something they could both build on—if they did it carefully?

CHAPTER SEVEN

'DO YOU WANT to know if it's a girl or a boy?'

Noah felt his breath catch somewhere deep in his chest. No. He didn't want to know. This was hard enough, sitting in this dim room with the ultrasound technician on the other side of the bed Abby was lying on. He hadn't seen Abby lying down for weeks now and it was…poignant. He missed that closeness they'd had. That friendship that had been strong enough to allow intimacy.

He had focused on the screen as soon as the scan had been started but he watched it with a clinical interest as he tried to make sense of the blobs that came in and out of focus. That was the head, of course…and there was the line of tiny vertebrae that made up the spine…

'I think I do,' Abby said. 'What about you, Noah?'

It didn't matter what he thought. This was about Abby. About supporting her in whatever way he could.

'Up to you,' he said. 'It might make it easier to… I don't know…think about names or what you'll need in the way of baby clothes.'

He and Ellen had known they were having a girl. There'd been a huge box of tiny pink clothes to donate to a charity when he'd finally cleaned out their house to move away.

Abby's head swivelled back towards the technician. 'Can you tell?' she asked.

'Sometimes it's easy.' She nodded. 'If it isn't it could be either because baby might have his legs crossed but when he hasn't…'

'So it's a boy?'

'It is.'

'Oh…' Abby's gaze was riveted to the screen so she didn't see that Noah had to close his eyes to absorb this piece of news.

A boy.

His son…

He opened them as the technician moved the transducer to focus on the baby's heart.

'Here's the cross-section, four-chamber view of baby's heart. I'll turn on the sound so you can hear it, too.'

Abby gasped as the sound filled the small room. And then she grinned. 'Sounds like a dog's chew toy after the squeaker's broken,' she said. But when her gaze slid away from the screen to catch Noah's, he could see something that was very different to humour in her eyes.

He knew exactly what it was that had brought Abby to the verge of tears because he'd felt it himself that first time. The absolute wonder of a glimpse into a new life that was forming. A new person. Their *child*... Noah was braced for a flashback and needing to distance himself for protection but something else seemed to be happening in his head—and his heart?

This was different.

New ground. Not just because this was Abby he was with and not Ellen. Not just because the baby was a boy and not a girl. Maybe it felt so different because he was standing back and it felt like he was watching this happening to someone else through a barrier but there was a thread of something that he might be able to catch—like when you were trying to remember something that had happened in a dream. Noah wasn't sure what it was but he did know it was worth catching. It was something good.

'I'll turn on the Doppler,' the technician said, 'so we can see the direction of blood flow in the heart.' Coloured blobs now appeared on the screen, moving in time to the rapid beat. 'No obvious turbulence or reverse flow,' she said moments later. 'And nothing crossing the septum. It's all looking reassuringly normal.'

Normal…

That had something to do with whatever nebulous feeling Noah had been aware of.

A normal family?

He was still pondering the odd mix of feelings the appointment had generated when he was walking beside Abby as they left the ultrasound section of St John's X-ray department.

He could feel a new—strong—connection to Abby now. A connection to the tiny being whose heart function he'd just been watching. His son. Abby was the mother of his son, which made them…a family.

And families should be together if that was at all possible.

He could make it possible. Only this morning, he'd been idly clicking through offerings on a real estate website as he'd eaten his breakfast and he'd come across a house that was not far away from where Lisa and Hugh lived. Abby's extended family. A real house, not an apartment. With a garden that was big enough for a small child to have adventures in. He could make an appointment to view the house. He could take Abby with him to see what kind of changes would need to be made to make it wheelchair friendly. They could make it work. Couldn't they?

The doors of the lift slid shut after the only other person got out at the next floor.

'Abby?'

She tilted her head up, her eyebrows raised in a question mark.

Noah took a deep breath. 'I think we should get married.'

'Oh, my God… He asked you to *marry* him? Noah *proposed* to you?'

'Not exactly. He said he thought we *should* get married. That he'd found a house not far from here where we could all live together happily ever after.'

The ironic tone in Abby's voice made Lisa's heart sink. 'So what did *you* say?'

'Well…nothing right then. Someone else got into the lift. But we went for a walk outside. In that strip of park behind the hospital that's got that creek running through it. I've never spent much time there because the paths aren't great for wheels but it's really quite pretty. There are daffodils out at the moment.'

Lisa's nod was impatient. 'I don't want to hear about the scenery…' She adjusted baby Amy in her arms so that she could latch onto her other breast. 'I want to know whether we're planning for a wedding as well as a new baby in the family.'

'No…' Abby made it sound as if she'd asked an obviously stupid question. 'Of course not.'

Making sure Amy was latched on and sucking properly was a good excuse not to say anything for the moment. To weigh up whether she should say what was becoming an increasing concern to both herself and Hugh—that the change in Abby's *joie de vivre* in recent weeks had more to do with Noah's distance than adapting to a major life change or the inevitable challenges that motherhood was going to present.

'*We're not a couple,*' she'd been telling them right from the start. '*We're just friends and it's never going to be more than that. And, yeah, we're having a baby together, but that makes it good that we're friends. Better than being strangers or bitter divorcées, yes? Much easier, if you ask me.*'

But Lisa wasn't so sure about that. Because she knew her sister.

'Talk to me, hon,' she said softly. 'Is it such a bad idea to marry someone that you're in love with?'

Abby's jaw dropped. 'I never said I was in love with him.'

'You didn't need to.' Lisa could feel the weight of the baby changing in her arms as Amy slid into sleep. She moved her daughter so that she was upright on her shoulder and began to rub her back. 'I know what it feels like, remember? I was in love with Hugh and then we split up and I had worst weeks of my life. I tried to convince myself that I'd get over him. That it was partly because

I was trying to get used to that new job and life would get back to normal eventually… and then you decided to sort things out.'

'Ha…' Abby shook her head. 'You were such a misery guts I had to do something. It was painfully obvious that you needed to be with Hugh and when he turned up on the doorstep, it was just as obvious he felt the same way. So that was when we hatched the plan to get you somewhere irresistibly romantic so he could tell you how he felt and persuade you to spend the rest of your life with him.'

'Maybe Noah feels the same way and he's just not ready to admit it. It took Hugh some time to realise how much he was missing me.'

Abby shook her head. 'We talked about that. I said that having a baby together wasn't a good enough reason to get married. That I couldn't marry someone that wasn't in love with me. And he said…' Abby paused for a moment to clear her throat and take a new breath—as if she was fighting off tears. 'He said that he couldn't offer that. To anyone. Ever. That he believes that he's not capable of feeling like that ever again but…but that he does care. A lot. That he would do his best to be a great husband. And father. That…um…friendship was actually a good base for any kind of long-term relationship and that maybe it would last longer than a lot of marriages.' A sound that was halfway between a sob and laughter escaped. 'Especially when the sex was great…'

'Oh… Abby…' A piece of Lisa's heart was breaking. She'd only ever wanted happiness for her sister and Abby had tackled every challenge in her life with such determination and good humour. She so deserved to be in the happiest part of her life, like Lisa was. 'It's not enough, though, is it?'

Abby shook her head. 'It would be settling for something less than ideal, that's for sure. I suspect it would eventually destroy whatever friendship we've got. We might end up hating each other.'

Lisa's sigh was heartfelt. 'You deserve so much more than that. You need someone that's going to totally adore you. Someone who can't live without you any more than you want to live without him.'

Abby nodded this time as a tear escaped and rolled down her cheek. 'Like you and

Hugh,' she whispered. 'But that's never going to happen.'

'You don't know that.'

'But I do.' Abby's eyes were shimmering with more tears. 'Because I can't imagine feeling like this about anyone else. And it's *Noah's* baby that I'm having. No one else could ever be the real father.'

Baby Amy chose that moment to release a loud burp and this time it was a genuine huff of laughter that came from Abby.

'You said it, Amy.' She was still smiling through her tears as she reached out. 'Enough self-pity,' she announced. 'It's time I had a cuddle. I haven't even told you the most important thing that happened at that scan. We found out that Amy's getting a boy cousin. I hope she doesn't boss him around as much as you bossed me.'

'I never bossed you. You were far too bolshie to let that happen.'

Abby's inelegant sniff advertised that her tears were done with. 'Might have been better if I had let you be in charge, huh?'

The reference to what had caused Abby's disability in the first place—pulling her hand from her big sister's grasp and running into traffic—was a reminder of so many other things. Like the guilt Lisa had always carried that had made it difficult to step back far enough for both the sisters to forge their own futures.

But that had changed in the last couple of years. She had met and fallen in love with Hugh. Abby had embraced her independence and her life had been an inspiration for any young woman, disabled or not. But now she had met and fallen in love with Noah and was faced with a future as a single parent. What were the chances that Abby's future could end up being as happy as Lisa's?

She handed over her baby. A cuddle was definitely what Abby needed. She just wished there was more she could do. She looked at her sister's head bent over her niece and could imagine that she would look just like this in a few months, holding her own infant. Only she would be looking even more beautiful bathed in that unbelievable glow that came from nowhere as you held your own baby for the very first time. Surely that would melt whatever barriers Noah Baxter had around his heart if that was what was keeping him from giving Abby what she needed?

Because broken hearts *could* heal. Sometimes, though, she knew it felt safer to leave the bandages on and the only way of finding out whether healing had occurred was if they got ripped off, but that wasn't something that could be forced. It was generally up to fate as to whether it happened or it didn't happen and usually you didn't even see it coming because, if you did, you'd protect whatever it was that was safely cocooned beneath its bandages. It was only afterwards that you realised that it had happened.

Like falling in love could be for people who'd been hurt in the past.

Could seeing your baby be just as powerful?

Lisa could only hope so. That it might prove to be powerful enough to be the miracle that could dissolve the barriers that were fragmenting Abby's life.

Things were coming together.

Slowly but surely.

A bit like the surgery Noah was completing, the crick in his neck and having to blink away blurriness occasionally as he peered through the magnifying glasses, letting him know that he'd almost reached his limit for the precise and painstaking reattachment of nerves, blood vessels and tendons in the small hand on the table in front of him as he reattached the ends of two fingers that had been amputated by a door.

The poor mother of this child had had no idea the three-year-old girl had poked her fingers into the crack and that, by opening the door further, she had caused the horrific damage. She was always going to feel guilty, even though it could never have been deliberate, but Noah could help by doing the best job he could in attaching the fingertips and children were amazing in the way they could heal. There would be scars, of course, but he was confident that, in years to come, the function of these tiny fingers would be just as good as if the accident had never happened.

Would the mother's guilt fade as well?

Noah could strip off the headpiece as his registrars took over the splinting and bandaging of the hand and the anaesthetist began to reverse the anaesthetic. It was only then, as Noah could see things that weren't magnified enough to let him work on precise structures that would have been invisible to the naked eye, that he realised what a beautiful child this little girl was, with her tumble of golden curls and dark lashes that lay on chubby, pink cheeks.

Three years old.

The age his own daughter would have been if she'd lived.

Not that Noah let himself think of things like that for more than a microsecond. Or even let them become anything more that something that was registered in a deep part of his brain—like a newspaper headline when you had no intention of reading the article beneath. He knew how to cope. He simply focused on something else. Something immediate and real. It was a form of mindfulness that worked well.

'Leave the tips of the fingers completely exposed,' he told his registrar. 'We need to be able to check the colour and temperature and capillary refill in the nail beds. Let's top up the hand block as well. I don't want her in too much pain when she wakes up. I'm going to go and talk to the parents.'

Noah checked the wall clock as he left Theatre. He still had time to get to his appointment and then make it to his dinner date with Abby. Not that it was any kind of "date", of course. They hadn't even kissed since they'd found out about the pregnancy.

It had taken months to even get to a point where friendship wasn't strained and awkward but it was finally happening and Noah knew it had a lot to do with his modus operandi. The mindfulness of having a focus that was real. Palpable. Preferably with a time limit that meant it needed constant attention, like the huge project he'd taken on in the last few weeks when he'd finally taken possession of the house he'd purchased after Abby had refused to consider his offer of marriage.

'You don't have to live in it,' he'd told her. 'But we're going to be co-parenting and I want you to be able to visit comfortably so I need your input for the changes that need to be made. I need the name of the architect you used to renovate your apartment, too, because I want this house to feel like that. Like…home…'

The appointment this evening was to get

the plans the architect had drawn up and then it was his turn to provide dinner at Abby's place. He'd found a new range of ready-made meals and it felt good to be tapping back into something that had given them another connection in the first place. A block that was the same but different and one that might fill another gap in the foundation of the friendship they were rebuilding.

It was also something so tangible it could be tasted, which made it as good as the paper plans they would have to focus on to discuss. It wasn't that he was trying to avoid emotional involvement or anything, it was just being practical. Being positive and taking one step after another into the future without letting something get in the way—like being dragged back into a past that no longer existed.

Like concentrating on being able to see those tiny fingertips that needed to heal instead of thinking about a little girl who had never had the chance to grow up. Planning practical changes to a house so that someone in a wheelchair could navigate easily between rooms and even floors, and not think of how different things could have been if his life had stayed on track. Supplying a meal that would hopefully tempt Abby to eat properly because she'd been looking a bit too pale and tired when he'd seen her in the hand clinic a couple of days ago.

He'd waited until Steve had shown him just how much progress he was making with his new thumb and had shared the exciting news that he was starting work again next week, but when he'd left her office, Abby had brushed off his concerns by telling him she was fine. She always said that, though, didn't she? Abby was more of a master than he was in finding positive things to focus on and facing any twists and turns in her life with the kind of courage he wished he had in such abundance. It was one of the things he admired so much about her but it could be a barrier as well.

He had the distinct feeling there were things going on that she simply didn't want to talk about but he was hardly in a position to expect more when they were still finding their feet in a new relationship. A friendship without the "benefits". Two people that needed to find a way of being able to be parents together when the changes were derailing the lives they had both been living.

But it felt like things were finally coming together.

Maybe tonight they could find their way back to a level where they could really talk about things. The way they had that night, which seemed for ever ago, when they'd both talked about how they didn't think it would be possible for them to make love to anyone.

That was ironic enough to make Noah smile but there was sadness mixed in with the amusement. Life could change in a heartbeat, couldn't it? With a trip on a staircase. Or a kiss that just made you want more. That gave you a glimpse of everything you'd ever wanted but knew you couldn't have any more.

Oh…man…

Sometimes the mindfulness thing didn't work so well. It was just as well he could see his young patient's parents in the relatives' room outside Theatre now. And they'd seen him. They were on their feet and they looked terrified.

His smile was reassuring this time, with no hint of any sadness.

'Good news,' were his first words. 'It's all gone just as well as we could have hoped.'

'He's thought of everything.'

Noah's smile was bright enough to be almost a beam but Abby couldn't return it with anything like such enthusiasm. She was getting used to the way the elephant in the room could be ignored and she knew that Noah was only looking this happy because he had something to talk about that had nothing to do with the baby.

'Look at this. Lowered workspaces in the kitchen and laundry.'

'You're over six feet tall, Noah. You should be having your workspaces raised, not lowered. I hope you realise that I'm not planning to come over and do your laundry anytime soon.'

Oh, dear... Abby knew she sounded tetchy but, dammit, she was feeling tetchy this evening. It wasn't so much the elephant in the corner of the room right now—it was more that elephant that was pressing on her bladder.

'Excuse me... I need to go to the loo.'

It was the second time she had ducked off

to the bathroom since Noah had arrived and taken over, putting the foil-covered boxes from the latest gourmet ready-made meal service he had discovered into the oven and then spreading the architect's detailed plans all over the kitchen table.

The worst thing was that this house that Noah was about to spend a fortune on to make wheelchair friendly was a smaller version of the rural mansion that Lisa and Hugh lived in. A perfect family home. The kind Abby would have dreamed of living in, if things were different.

But they weren't different. Okay, she and Noah might be in a better space now, having had more than three months to get used to the idea of becoming parents, but they were never going to recapture the kind of connection that they'd found when their friendship had begun. By the time she came back from the bathroom, Noah's smile had vanished completely and she could tell he was treading carefully again.

'I don't expect you to do any laundry,' he told her. 'I'm quite happy to have a housekeeper available but I'm just thinking of the future. I don't expect you to give up a career you love and I certainly don't want to give up mine.'

'I don't see what that's got to do with the height of worktops in your house.'

'What if I want to go to a conference sometime? And it's your turn to do the child-care but it's better to be at my house because it's closer to his school or he's got a hut in the garden that he likes to play in. And he gets muddy and you want to throw his clothes in the wash. Or cook him dinner.'

Abby was staring at Noah. 'Why is he always "him" or "he" when you talk about our baby?'

'Ah…because he's a boy?'

'He needs a name.'

That shut Noah up. Abby could see the shutters come down in his eyes. He'd flatly refused to discuss any choice of names because he said it was far too early and, anyway, he'd be happy to go along with whatever she chose, but sometimes it was better to wait and see what a baby's personality might be like.

Why wasn't it enough that her baby's father was committed enough to be planning for the future with such thoroughness being given to every possible scenario? Because it was at the kind of superficial level that came from someone keeping an emotional distance?

They'd talked about houses and gardens and childcare and schools—everything that could be needed to provide for a child's happy upbringing except for what their baby needed the most. Parents who loved each other as well as their child. It should be getting easier to get used to this but, if anything, it was getting harder.

There were moments when Abby wondered if she'd made a huge mistake in dismissing the idea that she and Noah could get married and live together to raise their little boy. It would be better than this, wouldn't it? This…longing to be touched. To be cherished…and becoming more and more aware of the distance between them.

Maybe it was pregnancy hormones getting to her. Of course it wouldn't be better. It would be soul destroying to live with someone and love them as much as she loved Noah and to be reminded, every single day, that she could never take the place of the woman he had truly loved. And she was tired as well. The extra weight Abby was carrying was making everything harder, even a simple transfer from her chair to her car or bed or a couch, but she needed to change her position more frequently because there were some pressure areas on her skin that her medical team were concerned about. So she was moody and sore and tired and Noah didn't deserve to be on the receiving end of it all.

'Sorry,' she muttered. 'It's been a long day.'

'You must be hungry. I reckon you'll like what I found today at Gourmet to Go.' Noah stood up and moved to the bench to picked up the discarded wrapping for the foil packages in the oven. 'How good does this sound? Chargrilled organic chicken breasts in a red pepper sauce, served on mushroom risotto with a side of green beans cooked to al dente perfection?'

'Mmm…' Abby tried to sound appreciative, even though she didn't feel at all hungry.

'Okay…' Noah was giving her that intense look, as if he was trying to decide whether something was wrong. 'There's a salted caramel crème brûlée for dessert if that's more exciting.'

'Sorry. I'm not very hungry, that's all.' Abby had her hand on her belly—an automatic reaction to feeling her baby move. She knew better than to offer to let Noah feel that movement—not after it had been dismissed in the past with the same kind of denial that discussing baby names had received.

This didn't feel like a normal sort of kick or wriggle—everything suddenly felt oddly tight—but then her ability to feel in her lower body wasn't exactly normal either, was it? It was probably just her bladder complaining again. It certainly felt as if she needed another trip to the bathroom. Or, oh… God… was it too late?

Noah had seen the expression on her face. 'What's wrong?'

'I…um… It's nothing… I just need to go to the loo again.'

But Noah was in front of her chair as she started to move. 'This isn't normal,' he said. 'What's going on?'

He put his hand on Abby's forehead and it felt deliciously cool but Noah swore softly.

'You're burning up,' he said. 'No wonder you look so tired. You're *sick*…'

'It's probably just a virus.'

'You've been running off to the loo every ten minutes. Sounds more like a UTI to me.'

Abby closed her eyes. 'You could be right,' she murmured. 'I did wonder if it smelt funny the last time.'

Noah flicked the switch off on the oven. 'We're taking you into ED,' he said. 'You need to be checked and started on some antibiotics.'

'I need some clean clothes. I'm…a bit wet.'

Even as she said the words, Abby realised it was an understatement. She was more than "a bit wet". There was fluid dripping from the cushion of her chair to puddle on the floor. Too much fluid for it to be coming from a very recently emptied bladder.

Noah was clearly thinking the same thing, but if he was worried it wasn't showing on his face. Abby had never seen him look quite this calm.

'I'm calling an ambulance,' he told her. 'I think your waters have just broken.'

CHAPTER EIGHT

'WHERE'S NOAH?'

'I saw him when we arrived.' Lisa bit her lip. 'He was talking to one of the doctors in the ward reception area. I overhead mention of…um…was it magnesium sulphate?'

Hugh nodded. 'They're planning to add it into what they're giving Abby to try and slow down or prevent premature labour. It's been shown to protect brain development and reduces the risk of complications like cerebral palsy.'

Abby closed her eyes. This nightmare wasn't going to go away anytime soon. The drugs she was being given to slow her contractions didn't seem to be working either. And now the beeping of the monitor beside her bed that was recording the baby's heart rate seemed to be slowing down when her belly tightened for longer periods.

Hugh was watching the monitor. 'You've had the second of the corticosteroid injections to help baby's lung development, yes? It's been more than twelve hours since you came in.'

Abby nodded. 'Why?' She fixed her gaze on her brother-in-law. 'You think I'm going to deliver this baby, don't you?'

'You need to be prepared for that.'

'But it's too early. I'm only twenty-nine weeks.' Abby was fighting tears. 'This is my fault. I should have picked up on the signs of a UTI. If I'd started antibiotics earlier, this might not be happening.'

'This isn't your fault, Abby.' Lisa took hold of her sister's hand. 'And you're in the best place you could be. St John's neonatal intensive care unit is second to none and… and babies survive way before twenty-nine weeks these days.'

'She's right.' Hugh's voice was gentle. 'The odds are totally on your side. Your baby's got more than a ninety percent chance of making it if he is born now.'

But Abby couldn't stop her tears. 'But he's

not just my baby. He's Noah's baby too and…
and how can I ask him to be here when he's
already lost a premmie baby? Even if I really, really need him to be here…'

'You don't have to ask. I'm here, Abby.'

Everybody's gaze flicked towards a door
they hadn't heard opening. Behind Noah
stood the obstetrician in charge of the team
who had admitted her and there were other
staff members behind him. Because the information from the monitors in this room
had been transmitted to the central desk as
alarms had begun sounding?

Lisa and Hugh shared a worried glance.
'Do you want me to stay?' Lisa asked Abby.

Abby shook her head slowly, her gaze
fixed on Noah's as he walked towards her
bed. This was the person she needed with
her. The father of her baby who was about to
come into the world too soon. Someone who
could understand, only too well, how scared
she was at this moment. Maybe he was even
more scared because he knew what it was
like to go through something this traumatic
and yet he was here.

He was here for her and Abby had never

loved him more for being brave enough to
go through this again.

For giving her his hand to cling to as
things began happening around her and any
control had to be ceded to people who knew
what they were doing.

Lisa and Hugh slipped out of the room
as more people came in, pushing equipment
like an incubator and trollies and more monitors. Just minutes later, the only people here
with a connection that was more than professional were Abby and Noah, and it had to be
obvious to everyone how close their personal
connection was—they were holding hands
tightly enough for their knuckles to be white.

So many things were the same as Noah
watched what was happening a short time
later.

Those tiny limbs that looked as fragile as
twigs as they waved in the air in protest at
what so many people were doing to him as
they prepared to cannulate umbilical vessels and put the smallest size of breathing
tube down his throat. A chest that was so
small it was half covered by an ECG elec-
trode and the miniature ribcage so visible

with the struggle for each breath. The time it took to get the tube down that narrow airway and get the settings for the ventilator perfect. The woollen hat that looked five sizes too big that was slipping down over the baby's closed eyes as he was snuggled into the incubator. Wire after wire that came snaking away from that tiny body to be attached to every monitor available.

That sensation that something sharp was piercing his heart was the same, too. The knowledge that this tiny human was part of him. Was his *son*. And the fear was the same. Knowing all too well how precarious the next hours and days could prove to be for this new life. It was a fear that had to be somehow locked away securely enough for Noah to be able to stay strong. For Abby. And for the baby.

It helped that many things were so different at the same time.

He could focus on the fact that the mother of his child was not lying in front of him, having already lost her battle for life. Abby was very much alive, still hanging onto his hand as if it was the only life belt on a terrifyingly rough sea. She had tears on her face but…yes…she had hope in her eyes. And a love that was making them shine like nothing Noah had ever seen before. Of course it was love for the baby she had just brought into the world but when Abby looked up to catch his gaze, it felt like he was included in that love. Or could be, if he wanted to be.

Which he didn't. Or rather couldn't because that was what everybody really wanted, wasn't it? To be loved like that? But how could he let Abby feel this way about him if he couldn't offer her the same level of connection? Being loved could become a burden if it was one-sided and, if he couldn't feel the rush of that depth of feeling in this moment, it seemed unlikely that he ever would. Either it was still too soon for Noah or he'd been through something so traumatic he'd genuinely lost the ability to let go enough to love anyone like that.

And that was both heartbreaking but… kind of a relief at the same time because it meant that he could stay strong. That he could care very much but not be destroyed all over again if the worst happened.

'I'll go with him,' he told Abby, although he hadn't let go of her hand yet. Or maybe it was Abby who hadn't let go of his. 'They're going to take him to NICU now.'

She pulled her hand free. 'Go,' she agreed in a whisper. 'He needs one of us to be with him. Just…' Another tear rolled down her cheek. 'Just…in case…'

Noah wanted to stay. Not just because he couldn't quite suppress the flash of fear at the thought of being present as the only parent if the worst happened. He wanted to stay here to make sure that Abby was being well looked after. To try and comfort her in some way and reassure her if he could. To care for *her*. Because he could this time? Because she was still alive?

But part of him knew he had to be with that tiny scrap of humanity that was their child, no matter how hard it was.

His head was such a mess that the only way he could take control was to take all those feelings and push them back. To slam a door on them and then lean on it with enough force to stop these confused thoughts and feelings that were so powerful, it almost felt as if he was physically being torn in two.

Oddly, though, it felt like Abby was still holding his hand as he followed the medical team surrounding the incubator out of the room. And it did kind of feel like a life belt and he certainly needed one. This was history repeating itself in the worst possible way. Was this another life that was going to be measured in no more than hours?

The first forty-eight hours should have been the hardest.

Abby knew that every time Noah came to the NICU where she was sitting, hour after hour, beside their baby's incubator that he had to be remembering the last time he'd done this. That he was probably reliving the tragic finale to that terrible time. When two days became three and then four and finally a week—when some of the wires and tubes had gone and she was expressing breast milk every few hours so that it could be fed to her baby, Abby had expected the tension might ease a little but, instead, it was getting worse.

She had turned her wheelchair to the wall this evening because she had discovered it was the best way to feel as if she and her baby were alone and as close as they were allowed to be. Abby still hadn't been able to hold him in her arms but she could do this—she could put her hand through the porthole of the incubator and put her fingertip on the palm of that tiny hand and let him close his fingers and hold on—the tiniest fingers imaginable but they could hold on with a strength that never failed to give Abby hope. That made her love him more and more with every passing day they were together.

Facing away from the rest of a unit that was busy but carefully quiet and without harsh lighting to protect these vulnerable babies meant that Abby didn't see Noah come in but she was aware of the change in how the space around her felt. Because she was getting used to him coming in at this time of day, when his work responsibilities were dealt with, or was it deeper than that in that it somehow felt safer when he was here—as if their baby could get more strength by having both his parents nearby?

Abby didn't move. She kept her gaze on that tiny hand still gripping her fingertip but in her peripheral vision she could see the movement of her baby's chest wall, and knowing how hard he was still working to breathe made it hard to keep the wobble out of her words. Behind that was a blur of golden fabric—a soft security blanket that had a small, toy lion and its front paws attached to one corner. The cuddly blanket stood out as one of the only personal items amongst all the medical paraphernalia.

'Did they show you the test results? The echocardiogram and the ECG?'

'Yes.' Noah positioned a chair beside Abby and sat down. He rested a hand on the top of the incubator and leaned closer, as if he was trying to see their baby through the jumble of wires and tubes and sticky tape and the oversized hat and nappy. 'A patent ductus arteriosus is not an uncommon heart defect in premature babies. It only becomes a significant problem if enough blood is bypassing the lungs to reduce the flow to the rest of the body, which can damage other organs like the intestines and kidneys.'

'If the medications don't help it close, they're talking about him needing surgery.'

'I know.' Noah was quiet for a moment. 'But it's a procedure that can be done by catheter now, even for someone as little as this. That wouldn't be nearly as scary as open chest surgery.'

It was Abby's turn to say nothing. It would still be terrifying.

Inside the incubator the baby moved, stretching legs so that his tiny feet were in the air. One hand also rose but the other was still gripping Abby's finger.

'Look at that,' Noah said softly. 'He's not letting go, is he?'

'He's a wee fighter,' Abby whispered back. She blinked back a tear, shifting her line of vision to the soft toy in the corner of the incubator. 'Our wee lion.'

The silence was longer this time. Until Abby audibly caught her breath which made Noah catch her gaze.

'Leo,' she murmured. 'It's the perfect name for him, isn't it?'

He was a week old but the name tag on the wall behind him still read simply 'Baby Phillips/Baxter' and there'd been too much else to think and feel and worry about to make choosing a name a priority. Especially when Abby knew that it had been something Noah had wanted to avoid. Even now, his gaze was sliding away from hers and she could feel the way his body was tensing—preparing for him to get up and go?

'You said that sometimes it was better to wait and see what a baby's personality was like, remember?'

Noah was nodding slowly but he was still starting to move away.

'Leo.' It sounded like he was testing the name as he looked down at the baby. Abby could see the muscles in his throat move as he swallowed. 'Yes…it's perfect.' But he glanced at his watch. 'I've got a patient I should check on. I'll have to go.'

Abby couldn't keep the wobble from her voice this time. 'Me, too. I… I have to go home tonight. Apparently I'm too well to have a bed in the ward now.'

'Oh…'

Noah clearly understood how hard it was going to be to become like the other parents in the unit who could only come in to spend the day with their babies, even if that day could stretch to ten or twelve hours.

'Are you going to stay with your sister?'

'She suggested that but I'd rather be in my own home where things are, you know…a bit easier. Lisa offered to stay with me there but she's busy with Amy and I don't want to wear her out.' Reluctantly, Abby was disengaging her finger and taking her hand away from the warmth inside the incubator. 'It's not as if this is going to be over anytime soon and I might need her even more later.'

'Let me help,' Noah said. 'I could come home with you and…and cook dinner, at least.'

Oh…there it was, just for a heartbeat. That silent communication that seemed to have vanished behind some kind of barrier a long time ago—about the time that Abby had discovered she was pregnant? Anyway…it was still there—just well hidden. This flash of connection acknowledged the only "cooking" either of them was likely to do was to turn on the oven to heat food that someone else had prepared far more expertly than they could.

Not that Abby felt remotely hungry but the offer was too good to turn down because it would provide what she needed far more than food and that was the company of the man she loved. The father of the baby she loved and who now, finally, had a name that they had chosen together and it made it feel as if they were even more of a family. A family that couldn't be together for more than fractured moments but every one of those moments felt too precious to waste right now.

'I'd love that,' she told Noah. 'I'll go and pack up my stuff in the ward. Come and find me when you're ready to go home.'

Home...

That's what it felt like, following Abby through the front door of her apartment. A comfortable, familiar space that he liked to be in. With a person he liked to be with. It was good to have something to do as well. To put a meal together from the wealth of supplies he found in both the fridge and the freezer.

'Someone's been shopping for you. And they cleaned up the food we left in the oven the night that... Leo decided he was going to arrive early.'

It felt strange to say their baby's chosen name aloud again. Who would have thought that a name could be powerful enough to change something that felt huge. Scary even... Just three letters but it made his son more *real*, somehow. A small person with a name that reflected his courage.

'Lisa's been in and out.' Abby told him.

'She had to come and get things I needed, like fresh clothes. And I wanted something to go in Leo's incubator right from the start so it didn't look quite so clinical. I'd bought that lion lovey blanket ages ago to give to Amy but then I kept it because I thought it was so cute. I hid it away because... I don't know...maybe I knew how much I wanted to have a baby one day.'

She hadn't planned on having one this soon, though, had she? Or with someone who couldn't give her the kind of love she absolutely deserved. There was a heavy feeling in Noah's chest, like a stone that was gradually getting bigger, but he tried to ignore it and stay cheerful. Supportive.

'Maybe we should go with a lion theme for his nursery?'

'It might be a good idea in your house. To go with that jungle of a garden you've got out the back.'

This made where he was feel less like home. There was a jarring note to be found in thinking about separate living arrangements that needed to be made but...that was the way things were, wasn't it? As much a part of what they were dealing with as the fact that he couldn't offer what he felt he should be able to offer to the mother of his child.

Abby was coping somehow so Noah had to follow her example, that was all there was to it. He mentally added finding a landscape gardener to the list of things he needed to get organised. He would give the go-ahead to start the alterations to his new house in the next few days as well, he decided, as he collected the plans still scattered on Abby's kitchen table. The more he had to supervise, or better yet to do himself, the easier it would be to cope with the stress of what the next days or weeks might throw at them. And the better he could cope, the more he would be able to do to support Abby.

He only had to catch her gaze to see just how she needed him right now, no matter how bravely she was facing up to this new challenge in her life. This had to be the hardest part so far, being forced to be away from her baby, unable to reassure herself by listening to the steady beat of those monitors or the touch of his hand. She still looked far too pale. Too stressed. Too…scared.

He went to her and crouched down a little,

putting his hands on the wheels of her chair so that he wasn't looking down at her.

'How 'bout curling up on the couch for a bit? I'll go out and see if I can find some chips and gravy and mushy peas at the local chippie and we'll have a picnic on the coffee table.'

There was something warm in those gorgeous, soft, hazel brown eyes now. Gratitude that he was trying to do something that might make her feel better? No…it was more than that. It reminded him of the way she'd looked when he'd gone into the NICU this evening—when little Leo had been holding onto her finger. It was a look of love, that's what it was, and the longing to be able to feel that and gift it back to her was so strong it was actually a physical pain.

Or maybe the pain was coming not from a longing for something that he couldn't have but because he was hitting that barrier so hard. The one that made it impossible to feel that kind of love again because the flip side of that coin was a loss that was too unbearable to risk. Whatever…his heart was aching. For himself but more for Abby, and without thinking Noah offered his arms. It was a reflex action, wasn't it—to find something physical to do in order to strengthen whatever protection was needed from something emotional? Abby, surprisingly, accepted his silent offer to carry her to the couch so that she didn't have to make the effort of moving and transferring herself. She lifted her own arms and wrapped them around his neck as he lifted her body.

Holding Abby in his arms hadn't been his brightest idea, though. To feel the shape of her body against his, the warmth of her skin—the scent that was uniquely Abby's—was too much of a reminder of how close they had been back in the days when it had seemed safe because they had only been "good friends". But nothing was really safe, was it? And he might be doing his best for both Abby and his son at the moment but Noah felt like a failure.

They both needed more from him and he simply didn't have it to give. And this wasn't fair. On any of them.

'I'm sorry,' he murmured, as he put Abby gently down on the soft cushions of the couch. It had been this couch where they'd made love that first time, which only made the memories stronger and increased the guilt that he'd made a serious error of judgement that was going to affect the lives of other people as well as himself. Abby deserved so much more than Noah could offer.

'What for?'

Noah had already turned away, fishing in his pocket for his car keys. He looked back just long enough to meet her gaze.

'Everything,' he said.

CHAPTER NINE

YOU COULD GET used to almost anything.

Like having to tap the sole of your baby's foot when the apnoea alarm sounded to warn that he'd stopped breathing for too long. Like making the most of the small things that you could do to help the nursing staff care for your baby, such as washing his face with the softest of muslin cloths or changing a disposable nappy that looked too big even though it was far smaller than any newborn size you could buy in a supermarket.

You could even get used to the roller-coaster of the hope that came with good news and the despair and fear that seemed to follow—sometimes only hours later. Things could change in a heartbeat—as they had today when Leo's apnoeic episodes had increased in frequency to the point that the decision had been made to go ahead with the surgery to correct his heart defect.

But even in a downward swoop of this journey, there could be a sudden, unexpected lift. A moment of pure joy, in fact. Like right now, when Abby was being allowed to actually hold Leo for the first time as they disconnected some of his monitors or changed them to a portable version so that he could be taken up to Theatre where his neonatal cardiology team were already preparing for his arrival.

"Holding" wasn't quite the right word for what she was doing, Abby thought. She had undone the buttons on her shirt and the nurses had lifted her precious baby from the incubator, expertly juggling wires and tubes to prevent tangling, to place him onto her bare skin. He was just above her breasts, on his tummy with his arms and legs spread out and even his tiny fingers and toes splayed.

'He looks like a little tree frog,' Abby whispered. She touched his head with her finger so gently she could almost feel the individual hairs of the fluff covering his scalp. 'But you need to channel your inner lion, sweetheart. We've got stuff to get through today.'

'He's going to be fine.' Noah was right beside her. 'Did you understand everything they said about the procedure?'

'Not really,' Abby admitted. 'My training only included a fairly basic cardiac course and... I'm not sure it would help to know more. The idea that they're putting things into Leo's heart is terrifying enough.'

She was touching her baby's back now. Feeling the tiniest bumps of his spine. She could feel his heartbeat against her skin and it was all too easy to imagine just how tiny his heart was. How on earth could anyone repair something so small?

Of course Noah was confident. His whole life was spent operating on structures that were just as tiny. It was his passion but Abby couldn't understand why he wanted to talk about the procedure now, when he could be sharing the joy of this small miracle of being able to touch Leo properly for the first time. To count those tiny fingers and toes and touch the tip of his nose and marvel that something so small could be so utterly perfect.

But that was precisely why Noah was

seeking an escape, wasn't it? This felt like the hardest challenge Abby had ever faced but it had to be harder for Noah and she had to factor in that heartache to the emotional battle between joy and fear that was currently tumbling inside both her head and her heart as she soaked in every second of being this close to their baby.

'But maybe it would help,' she found herself saying. 'If you tell me again.'

If nothing else, Leo could listen to his father's voice for a few minutes. And Abby could stroke his soft, downy skin at the same time, to try and let him know just how much he was loved.

It was like being able to find a new handhold or somewhere to put your foot to take some of the weight that was threatening to make it impossible to climb this cliff and could send you tumbling God only knew how far or what was at the bottom.

This handhold was no more than a piece of paper and a pen but it provided something that Noah could focus on and, while he could still see their baby sprawled against Abby's much paler skin, it was only in the periphery of his vision and that was much easier to cope with.

His sketch was rapid but accurate enough to be useful and he was explaining at the same time as drawing the diagram.

'So this is the heart. You've got the two ventricles there, and the two atria on top and you've got these arteries, here… This is the pulmonary artery that takes deoxygenated blood from the right ventricle to the lungs and that's the aorta that takes the oxygenated blood from the left ventricle to the rest of the body. With me so far?'

He could see Abby's nod but she wasn't looking at him. Her gaze was firmly on Leo and she was touching one of his cheeks, softly tracing the outline of one of the strips of tape holding a tube in place—the nasogastric tube that was allowing him to be fed some of his mother's milk now, which was a step forward from only having intravenous nutrition.

'Before a baby's born, the lungs aren't going to be providing oxygen because they're full of fluid so the ductus arteriosus is an extra blood vessel that lets most of the blood go straight to the aorta and bypass the lungs. After birth, it closes up and becomes a ligament rather than a blood vessel. That's why it's a common problem with premmie babies and, if it's big enough, it can present significant issues, like it has with Leo.'

Noah paused to take a breath. He'd just made this suddenly so much more personal by using Leo's name instead of explaining something in terms of babies in general.

'But they're not going to cut his chest open, are they?' Abby's question was only a whisper but he could feel her fear hovering in the air between them.

'No. And he'll be sedated so he's not going to feel any pain. They'll make a very small incision to put a catheter into an artery in his groin and make sure it gets to exactly the right place in his heart by using X-rays to follow it. They can take measurements and pressure readings and then they can thread in another catheter that has a closure device on it. They position that and implant the device and it fills up the blood vessel and seals it shut.

'Then they take out the catheter, close the incision and make sure that there's no bleeding from the entry site. I'm not sure how long it will take and he'll need to go into a recovery area afterwards for close monitoring so it might be a while before you're back in here and able to hold him again.'

One of the nurses looked up from where she was adjusting settings on the incubator. 'It's nearly time to tuck him up again,' she said gently. 'His oxygen sats are dropping a bit. We'll probably get the call to take him up to Theatre soon, anyway.'

Abby was nodding. It looked like her lips were pressed together too tightly to let her say anything. She bent her head, just enough to touch the top of Leo's head with her lips and it seemed to startle him because he lifted his arms. One of the miniature miracles of a hand had come even closer to Noah and, without thinking, he lifted his own hand to touch it—as if he wanted to check that something so small and perfect could be real. He touched it just with the very tip of his forefinger on the palm of his son's hand but, almost instantly, Leo closed his hand and gripped Noah's fingertip in a tiny, determined little fist.

Noah froze.

It felt like time froze as well and the whole

world stopped turning for a heartbeat. And then another and another.

That, oh, so tiny hand was touching way more than Noah's fingertip. It was reaching inside his body. Into his heart. It was touching those walls he'd built so carefully to protect his heart and that touch was all it took for them to crack and begin to crumble. He could feel the cracks widening so that what was behind them was about to escape. A tsunami of...*feeling*...

Feeling the joy and hope and dreams of loving someone so much.

But also the fear that came with knowing what it would be like to have it all snatched away from you.

He could drown in that tsunami. But, even if he didn't drown, he would be swept off his feet and be unable to be strong for Abby while she faced up to her own fears as she waited for Leo to come out of Theatre. He caught her gaze at that moment, while his finger was still being held, and what he saw in her eyes was the final push on those walls.

He couldn't do this.

He couldn't *not* do this...

Noah had no idea what might have happened if his pager hadn't sounded right then. The loud sound was enough to startle Leo again and he let go of Noah's finger as the nurse carefully scooped him up from Abby's chest to put him back in his incubator.

'I...ah... I have to get this...' The pager message had come with a priority of something urgent.

Abby simply watched him as he got to his feet and moved towards a phone at the nurses' station to make an internal call. Noah's legs felt as if his whole body had been shaken by something and he could feel Abby's gaze following him. A curious gaze. Maybe a hopeful one? Was she wondering if she'd really seen what she'd thought she'd seen when his son had been holding his finger? That moment when he'd realised that it was only his own fear that was holding him back from loving someone absolutely. Not just Leo but Abby as well. *Especially* Abby...

The phone call was from the emergency department and Noah listened only for a very short time.

'I'm on my way,' he said.

A few rapid steps back towards Leo's corner of the NICU where he was being settled for when the call to transport him to Theatre came through. Abby had just put his woolly hat back on his head.

'I have to go,' Noah told her. 'I'm sorry. There's an emergency in ED. Someone's come in having split their hand in half with a circular saw.'

If there'd been anything like hope in Abby's gaze, it faded now into something very different. Resignation, maybe. Sadness? Or perhaps it was simply determination.

'We'll be fine,' she told him. 'Go. That person needs you.'

So did Abby and Leo. But Noah went— because he had to.

Because he needed to. Because this urgent summons was giving him the chance to escape and get to higher ground in the last moments before that tsunami arrived. A chance to take control back and, if he couldn't repair those protective walls in his heart, he could at least stay out of an overwhelming wash of emotions. He had to, because if that wave caught him, he might not be of any use to anyone and letting that happen would not only be selfish, it would be completely unacceptable. Someone was waiting for him in ED. Someone who was probably desperately hoping that Noah could help stop their injury from turning their world upside down for ever.

And he *could* do that. Or as much as it was possible to do and maybe, by doing that, he could save his own world from falling apart as well.

This waiting room was the loneliest place ever.

Lisa and Hugh were on their way to the hospital but they'd been in central London this morning, choosing Amy's first cot because, at nearly seven months old, she had grown too big for her bassinet and now they were caught in a traffic jam that didn't look like it was going to clear anytime soon.

Abby didn't know where Noah was. Probably scrubbing up for some incredibly long and challenging surgery to save his patient from losing his hand. The only thing that really mattered to her right now was that he wasn't here.

She was alone.

More alone than she'd ever been in her

life. She'd followed Leo's incubator as far as she was allowed—to the theatre anteroom where a specialist paediatric anaesthetist would be sedating her tiny baby so that he could undergo a procedure that might well be perfectly safe but it still seemed unbearably invasive, especially for a baby who wasn't even developed enough to be able to breathe on his own.

Rolling away from that room had felt like her heart was being ripped out and left behind. And now she had way too much time to sit here and feel that fear and the loneliness that was making it so much worse.

It was well over an hour since Noah had rushed out of the NICU to go to St John's emergency department but there'd been a delay in getting Leo up to Theatre. It hadn't been so hard waiting down in the unit because Leo was still safely enclosed in the plastic walls of his incubator and in the care of the amazing nursing staff who'd been watching over him almost from the moment he'd been born. So Abby had felt safe, too. More than that. She'd been able to sit there quietly with Leo, with her hand through the porthole and feel that exquisite pressure from the tiny fingers wrapped around hers.

The way he'd been holding his father's fingertip a short time ago.

And, oh… Abby could have sworn she'd seen straight through the barriers that Noah had kept up for as long as she'd known him. Straight through to a place where the glow of being able to love was shining so brightly it had almost blinded her for an instant. She'd seen a place that made her own heart break more than a little because it had dark corners where things like fear and tears lurked but the brightness of happiness and love and just…*hope*…could win if it was allowed to— for most of the time, if you were lucky— because it shone so much more brightly than the opposite side of that coin.

A member of staff from the surgical suite had been sent to keep Abby company in the waiting room but Abby had told her she'd rather be alone. It wasn't true, of course, but what she didn't want was to be with someone who didn't know her. Or Leo. Someone who had no understanding of just how agonising this waiting was, with every passing minute making it harder.

Why was it taking so long?

Had something gone wrong?

Why had she signed that consent form that had given them permission to do whatever might be needed if a complication arose— like opening up that tiny chest to do more major surgery?

Maybe that was what was happening right now. Abby could hear the footsteps of someone approaching this waiting area and they weren't the soft squeaky ones of the nurse who'd been wearing trainers. These steps sounded heavier. More urgent? Abby's heart was in her mouth as she turned to face the door and whatever bad news was on its way.

But the person filling the doorway was Noah and the expression on his face was… was as raw as she'd ever seen anybody look. Ever.

'I can't do it,' he said as he came towards her. He hunkered down so that his face was on the same level of Abby's and balanced himself by putting his hands on her wheels. 'I have to go and scrub up in a few minutes and I'll probably be in Theatre for hours but I had to come and tell you because, otherwise,

I don't think I could focus on what I need to do. So I came. To say that I can't do it.'

If Abby's heart had been breaking earlier, it was now in a million pieces that were raining down into a chasm so dark she didn't want to know how deep it was. She could get a sense of how deep it was, though, by what she could see in Noah's eyes. And she couldn't hate him for protecting his own heart. If she'd had a choice, she'd be protecting both his and Leo's from any of this.

'I know,' she said softly. 'I do understand, Noah. This is hard enough on me and I can see how impossible it would be to put yourself through it all over again.'

But Noah was frowning now.

'No...you don't understand, Abby.' Noah took hold of Abby's hands, which had been resting in her lap. 'What I can't do is *not* go through this. I can't not feel...*everything*. I can't *not* love Leo. Or you, Abby. It's been there all along but I couldn't reach it.' His eyes were shining with what looked very much like unshed tears. 'But something changed today and... I can feel it all. The fear and the pain but most of all... I can feel what it's like to love somebody this much and there's no going back from that. I can't be away from you—or Leo. I just can't do it.'

Those shattered pieces of Abby's heart were magically coming back together, as if someone had put a video on reverse and things were speeding backwards. It felt like there were more pieces than there'd been before, too, because her heart was feeling as if it wasn't going to stop getting bigger. As if it was so full it was in danger of bursting.

'I know how that feels,' she said, her voice cracking. 'I know exactly. Because it's how I feel about you. How I've felt for such a long time—before we even knew that Leo was on the way.'

Noah's arms were around her now. Holding her so tightly it was hard to breathe, but that didn't seem to matter. This was the only place that Abby needed to be at the moment. In Noah's arms, with her head tucked into that space beneath his collar bone, where she could hear, and feel, the steady beat of his heart. And feel his lips pressed against her hair and when he spoke she could hear the words but she could also feel them rumbling against her cheek.

'We'll get through this, Abby. Whatever

happens—now or in the future—we'll get through it together, okay?'

Abby could only nod. The promise in those words and her faith in that promise had made her throat too tight for her to breathe properly, let alone find any audible words.

She could hear someone saying something, though. A female voice. And now the weight of emotional overload made it seem as if it was too hard for her heart to keep beating as she looked up and saw the woman with a theatre gown still over her scrubs and a mask dangling by its strings around her neck. It was the cardiologist who'd been doing the procedure on Leo.

And she was smiling.

'It all went perfectly,' she told them. 'Your little boy came through with flying colours and he's absolutely fine. You can come and see him in Recovery.'

Abby turned at the exact moment Noah did and they held each other's, gaze which was far more intimate than handholding could ever be. And they both had tears escaping to dampen their cheeks. They were in this together and they always would be. And there was love there. So much love that Abby felt sure that even if there were darker things to face in the future, the glow from that kind of love would never be extinguished.

They were together now, she and Noah. As committed as any couple could ever be.

More than that, it really felt like they were a family already.

And it was time to go and see their son, even if it would only be for a minute or two on Noah's part because he had an important job to go and do. Other people needed him as much as Abby and Leo did. They needed him more right now, in fact, and that was okay because Abby and Leo and Noah had the rest of their lives ahead of them to be together as much as possible.

And even if they weren't in the same room together, that love would still be there and Abby knew it was going to keep her as strong as she needed to be until they could take their baby home.

CHAPTER TEN

FACING CHALLENGES IN life with another person always held a risk that it could test a relationship too much and force you apart, but a tough patch could also do the opposite and build a foundation that felt like it would be strong enough to withstand anything and everything that life could throw at it in the future.

Getting stronger was exactly what the next ten weeks did for Abby and Noah as they lived their lives centred on the neonatal intensive care unit until baby Leo was big and strong enough to go home.

There were milestones along the way that neither of them would ever forget, even if they didn't have some special photographs that had captured the memories—such as the day Leo had been able to come off the ventilator and breathe for himself after the corrective surgery on his heart meant that his condition had improved enough so he'd only needed some supplementary oxygen.

It was Noah who was holding him this time. Sitting with his shirt open so that he could have skin-to-skin bonding time with his son, leaning back in his armchair so that Leo was lying flat with his arms and legs out—doing what Abby called his little tree frog impression. Abby had positioned her wheelchair as closely as possible to where Noah was sitting because, that way, she could touch both of them, with a hand resting on Noah's leg and the palm of her other hand taking the weight of Leo's tiny foot with those precious little toes.

It wasn't just that their baby was almost hidden by being cupped by Noah's hand. Or that he had his eyes open and seemed to be not only taking in everything that was happening around him but content in knowing how much he was loved.

For Abby, this was filling her heart even more because, despite still being in the unit, this was one of those deeply private experiences that was bringing her closer and closer to Noah every time they happened. She knew how significant this one was because she could see the tears in Noah's eyes.

Not like that night—in the early hours of the morning after Leo had had his heart surgery—when Noah had come home to Abby's apartment after spending such a long time in Theatre with the man who'd very nearly amputated half his hand. That day had been the turning point of their whole relationship— the day they'd become a family and one that had been baptised by many tears when they'd finally had the chance to be together properly. When Noah had come home simply to hold Abby in his arms.

To tell her how being able to love her was making him feel so many things all over again and he'd realised that maybe he'd never processed his grief properly all those years ago. Abby had encouraged him to tell her all about Ellen and she'd learned how they'd been so young when they'd met and how much they'd loved each other. He'd told her that, because Ellen had loved him that much, he knew that she would be happy that he'd found Abby and that she'd want him to love her and be loved in return. For them to be together to bring up their baby. And Abby had wrapped her arms even more tightly around them and promised that that was exactly what was going to happen and that they were going to make the most of every moment.

On this milestone, when Noah was holding Leo for the first time, there were more tears but they didn't need to share anything tragic. This was just something else that Noah needed to tell Abby about so that there were no secrets between them. No barriers to them being as close as it was possible for a couple to be.

'I was so scared to give him a name,' he said, so softly that nobody around them could hear. 'Ellen and I had chosen a name for our baby as soon as we found out she was on her way. We didn't tell anybody, though, and it was only at the very end, when I was holding her...like this...that I told them.'

Abby leaned sideways in her chair, so that she could rest her head against Noah's arm. So that he could tilt his head to touch hers. And they were both touching their baby, which made the connection so powerful that Abby's heart ached.

'What was it?' she whispered. 'Your daughter's name?'

'Grace.' Noah had to clear her throat. 'I spoke her name aloud and…just minutes later I lost her.'

Abby had to catch a tear with her fingers before it fell onto Leo.

'She's still part of you. Like Ellen is. And that makes them part of our family, too. We'll never forget them. Have you got photos?'

'Somewhere. Packed away like so many things were before I met you.'

'Let's find one. As soon as we've finished the painting in the house we'll start a family wall somewhere and we'll put them up. And…' Abby raised her voice a little as a nurse walked past the end of Leo's incubator. 'Jenny, have you got a moment to take a photo for us? Our first family photo?'

Leo learning to breastfeed was another milestone after a journey that began with no more than a lick and ended with him being able to latch on and suck for several minutes before tiring. The nasogastric tube that had been used to give him Abby's breastmilk for his early weeks was added to the growing pile of other tubes and monitoring wires that were no longer essential. Noah was by her side for that first proper feed and they had both been so happy with the progress.

'We'll be like normal parents in no time.' Noah had grinned. 'You'll be poking me when it's my turn to get up for a night feed.'

He was there for Leo's first smile as well, and happy didn't begin to cover how that made them both feel, even though there'd been no chance of capturing the moment in a photograph. It was enough to know that there would be many, many opportunities to do that in the months and years to come. They were both going to ensure that their tiny boy had plenty to smile about.

Moving out of Abby's apartment and into the house was a huge step forward into their new life together and, while the renovations were not quite complete, both Noah and Abby had wanted to be settled into their for ever home before Leo came out of the hospital. The photo taken that day was a selfie when they were finally alone in the house and they'd curled up together, exhausted, on one of the couches that had come from Abby's apartment.

'I still think we should have upgraded these couches,' she said. 'They're getting old.'

'Are you kidding? This couch has history and I'm keeping it for ever.' Noah pulled his phone from his pocket and held it above them to take a photograph.

'Oh…' Abby laughed. 'How could I forget that first time… I can't believe I actually confessed that I was a virgin when I hardly knew you.'

'And I still can't believe that you *were*. That somebody so incredibly beautiful and clever and kind and…well…pretty close to perfect really…hadn't already had her heart won.'

He dropped his phone and pulled Abby into his arms and kissed her. Such a long, slow, tender kiss that when she finally came up for air, it felt as though her bones had melted.

'I'm so lucky it was you,' she whispered. 'That you were my first. That I never need to go looking again because I know I'd never find anyone I could ever want to be with as much as you.'

The look in Noah's eyes as he got to his feet and gathered Abby into his arms made her completely forget how tired the moving in had made her.

'I think we need to check that they've put our bed in the right place, don't you?'

'Oh, yes...' Abby wrapped her arms more tightly around his neck. 'Absolutely.'

The glossiest photographs that were taken in the weeks before Leo finally came home weren't taken by Noah or Abby. Or even Leo's doting aunt and uncle on the many visits from Lisa and Hugh. They were photographs taken by a magazine and they weren't even the subjects of the article, although Steve and Pauline had tried to convince the journalist writing the article that Noah and Abby were the real heroes in the story of the toe that had become a thumb.

'It wouldn't have happened without both of them,' Steve told the journalist as they were grouped together for a photo. 'Dr Baxter for the incredible surgery he and team did for me. And Abby, of course. She kept me on track for all those early months and kept me going until I was good enough to get back to the job I love.'

Steve could see that the journalist was eyeing Abby with interest—as if she'd sensed another angle to the story she was writing.

'I know, right?' Steve nodded. 'Who wouldn't be inspired by a physiotherapist who knows what she's talking about because she's obviously been through more than a few challenges herself? I said that right from the start.'

'And you're still having therapy on your hand?'

'Nah… I'm pretty much discharged from care now. Unless I have a problem, of course. I'd be back like a shot to these two if that happened but I might have to wait until Abby's back at work and that might be a while from what we've heard.'

Pauline was smiling at Abby. 'We heard about your baby,' she said. 'That he arrived too early and that he needed an operation on his heart. That must have been so terrifying for you both.'

'It was,' Abby agreed. She couldn't help looking up to catch Noah's gaze. 'But we've got through it and Leo's doing really well. They're starting to talk about letting him come home.'

Noah was smiling back at her and the journalist and photographer exchanged glances themselves.

'So you're together?' she asked. 'You're married?'

'We're not married,' Abby responded. They could have been, of course, but she knew she'd done the right thing in refusing Noah's proposal when it had only been about being together as parents and not as two people who loved each other as well as their child. They'd been too busy since then, wrapped up in caring for their sick baby, work responsibilities and the renovations of their family home to even consider the idea of marriage again, and this question out of the blue made Abby think that if he asked her again, her answer might be very different.

Maybe she would ask him.

Or maybe they didn't need anything formal to advertise their commitment to each other.

'But we're definitely together,' Noah added.

He caught Abby's gaze again and it was her turn to smile.

'Yeah,' she murmured. 'Definitely together.'

'Did you meet at work?' The journalist had her notebook out again. 'It didn't have anything to do with Steve being your patient, did it? That would make such a lovely extra angle to this story.'

'Yes and no,' Abby admitted. 'It was Steve's first operation when I realised that Noah was St John's new specialist hand surgeon.'

'I knew there was something going on.' Pauline smiled. 'You could feel it in the air when they were in the same room together.'

'But we'd met before,' Noah added. 'And that hadn't had anything to do with Steve. You could say it was more of an accident than anything.'

'Oh?' The journalist looked eagerly towards Abby, hoping for more details.

Abby kept her face as straight as Noah's. Their story was their own and they weren't about to share it with the world at large. They weren't about to forget it either, however. An accidental meeting that was going to shape the rest of their lives.

So she simply shrugged as the silent communication between herself and Noah was
full of laughter. And love…

'It's no big deal,' she said. 'We just kind
of bumped into each other.'

EPILOGUE

One year later...

'This has to be the most romantic place on earth for a wedding.'

Abigail Phillips grinned at her sister. 'You should know. It's where you had yours. Where you got engaged *and* where you had your first date.'

'Mmm…' Lisa Phillips smiled dreamily into the mirror as she put the finishing touches to her hair. 'I'm just so happy to be back here. And for the best reason ever.'

'I was never intending to copy you. You know that, yes? I would have been more than happy to get married in the local registry office. It was Noah who had other ideas.'

'I'm pretty sure that was Hugh's doing. You remember that night you came around to dinner? When that magazine article had come out about that guy with the toe for a thumb and you told us that the journalist had assumed you were married?'

'Of course. And when we went out to the kitchen I told you that it didn't really bother me at all whether we got married or not. That I would always be happy as long as Noah and I were together.'

'Yeah…well, it was then that Hugh showed Noah the picture of where we got married. *This* place.'

'I know. He was still going on about it when we got home that night. The south of France, he kept saying. That view from that terrace. Those stone floors and walls…that grapevine…'

'It wasn't just the picture,' Lisa confessed. 'Hugh told me later that he'd told Noah that there was something magic about this particular restaurant. That it was only because he'd been clever enough to bring me here on our first date that I fell in love with him and we began our happy ever after.'

Abby laughed as she took the last sip of the glass of champagne she'd been given as she made her final preparations to marry the love of her life.

'It might be true. You *are* happy, aren't you?'

'Couldn't be happier. Especially now that the morning sickness is fading. I didn't get any the first time around with Amy. Hey... maybe that means it's going to be a boy this time. It would be nice for Leo to have a boy cousin.'

'Speaking of Leo. And Amy...it's about time we went to find my flower children, isn't it? If Hugh and Noah are playing with them, they're probably grubby already.'

'Let's see...'

Lisa gave Abby a searching glance from head to toe that took in her wheelchair with the tiny bunches of delicate, white gypsophila attached to the wheels' spokes with silk ribbons. Abby's dress was white and lacy but fitted enough to be elegant and she had a red sash around her waist to match her matron of honour's dress—a nod to the pact that the sisters had made when they were very young, that they would wear red despite the different shades of their hair because it was their happy colour. Abby's long, golden red hair was in loose waves, threaded with tiny white roses, fragrant orange blossom and single sprigs of gypsophila.

'Yep,' she pronounced. 'You're ready.' She looked around them. 'Where are the baskets of rose petals for the kids?'

'Over there. What's the bet that Leo just sits down and tries to eat them?'

Lisa smiled. 'They're edible. I checked.'

'Do you think he should be walking better by now?' Abby couldn't help the anxious question as they reached the door of the bathroom they'd been using for final preparations and she could see her son in his uncle's arms as he came towards them. 'Look at that. He still loves to be carried everywhere and he's nearly fifteen months old.'

'Don't forget he arrived nearly three months early so he's actually spot on with his milestones. Plus, he's the most adorable little boy in the entire world.'

Lisa stepped through the door to give Abby room to manoeuvre her wheelchair to the start of the aisle that had been created by shifting all the wrought-iron tables to one side of the terrace, where the wedding breakfast would be served later, and putting chairs—decorated with silk ribbons and more small clouds of the ethereal gypsophila—into rows for the select group of close friends and family who'd travelled to France to share this celebration.

Lisa smiled at her husband, who would be returning to his best man duties as soon as the children had been delivered back to their mothers to play their part in this intimate wedding ceremony.

'I should warn you, though…' she said, seriously. 'I can only keep saying that about Leo if it turns out that Amy's getting a little sister.'

Amy, at nearly two years old, was delighted with her task of being a flower girl and she was beaming as Lisa straightened her headband of white daisies and gave her the small, silk-lined basket of rose petals.

'You'll need to hold Leo's hand, sweetheart,' she told her daughter. 'You can go down to where Daddy and Uncle Noah are waiting and throw the petals on the ground on the way.'

'C'mon, Leo.' Amy turned to her cousin. 'Let's *go…*'

But Leo stayed where he was, standing there with his cute short trousers and braces over a white shirt with a red bow tie. And then he sat down on his well-padded rump and looked at his mother——those dark eyes looking huge in that perfect little face framed by dark waves just like his father's.

'You want a ride?'

Leo's face split into the biggest grin ever and he held up his arms. Abby laughed and expertly adjusted the position of her wheelchair so that she was close enough to lean over the side and scoop Leo into her lap.

Hugh was standing beside the groom now, in front of the stone wall of the terrace, where an archway covered with white flowers had been placed to offer the best possible view of the forests covering the mountainous terrain that flowed from this medieval French village towards the blue streak in the distance that was the Mediterranean.

Lisa walked ahead of Abby, helping Amy to scatter rose petals. Abby rolled across the big flagstones that made the floor uneven enough to bounce Leo on her lap and make him giggle. He hadn't been in the least bit upset that Lisa had taken his basket of petals to help Amy. He had his lion lovey blanket firmly in one hand, just in case he might need comfort in strange surroundings.

Not that he was looking anything less than

perfectly happy, cuddled against his mother as she approached the man who was waiting for them both.

Noah.

The man she always thought she couldn't possibly love any more than she did right now but then, almost every day, she discovered she was wrong.

Her lover.

Her best friend.

The father of her baby and now he was about to become her husband.

The enormity of it all stole Abby's breath away but that was okay. She'd never really needed words to be able to communicate with this man, had she?

She could tell him now just how much she loved him. And she knew, without a shadow of a doubt, that he would say exactly the same thing back.

* * * * *